Price Litner has been in and out of the military more times than he cares to remember. Every decade it becomes harder and harder to keep his vampire nature hidden. When a silly mistake drags his nature into question, Price knows he needs to find a safe place to lie low. He turns to the one man he can trust—ex-team member Graham Canton.

Even though Price is aware Graham lives at a marine park with a bunch of shifters, he knows he has no choice. He has to put his life in the hands of other paranormals—something he hasn't done in over one hundred fifty years. Price trusts Graham, so he takes the chance.

One of the men who accompanies the shifter pod alpha when he comes to question Price—after all, he could be bringing trouble their way—is none other than his beloved—a giant octopus shifter named Dare Winterwall. Can Price help the shifters save not only him but their anonymity, too? Oh, and will he be able to work past his queasiness of all things . . . tentacled?

Bobbing with a Giant Octopus
Copyright © 2021 Charlie Richards
ISBN: 978-1-4874-3279-9
Cover art by Angela Waters

Published by eXtasy Books Inc or
Devine Destinies, an imprint of eXtasy Books Inc

Look for us online at:
www.eXtasybooks.com or www.devinedestinies.com

Bobbing with a Giant Octopus
Beneath Aquatica's Waves
Book Ten

By

Charlie Richards

DEDICATION

Any entity — no matter how many tentacles it has — has a soul.
~Guy Consolmagno

CHAPTER ONE

Crouching on the roof of the apartment building across from where he'd been living for the past twelve years, Price Litner watched two vehicles marked military police pull up before his own structure. He would bet his fangs that there were more military police monitoring the back door, too. Price was certain they'd come prepared.

Just thirty minutes before, Price had been tipped off to their impending arrival. When he'd spotted Britt's message from a burner number, he'd frozen in disbelief . . . for all of two seconds. Then Price had pulled his head out of his ass and responded with a code meant to confirm Britt's identity.

As soon as Price had done that, Britt had called him. Without even a hello, he'd stated, "The military police are on their way to you. Get out."

Price hadn't asked the hows or whys—he'd just obeyed, grabbing his emergency go-bag and clearing from the apartment. Having known Britt for almost three decades, he had complete faith in the human. While the man didn't know he was a vampire, he'd always been a trustworthy friend.

Watching the four men in military uniforms pour from the vehicles, Price was damn grateful for his network of friends. He hadn't had a coven to depend on in over a hundred and fifty years—not since a lying donor had caused his master to banish him and name him rogue. That stigma had made it impossible to be accepted into another coven, so he'd gone it alone.

And I'd been doing just fine . . . until now. So what the hell happened?

Three of the men headed into the apartment. One waited outside. That one kept his hand on the butt of his service weapon as he peered all around the area. When the man began to tip his head back, Price ducked behind the wall and headed toward a fire escape on the far side.

Upon reaching it, Price peeked over the side and confirmed the coast was clear. He quickly scaled the ladder. Once his feet hit the ground, he used vampiric speed to take him down the alley, across a side street, and into a busy district full of cafes and shops.

Price spent fifteen minutes in that area, confirming that he didn't have a tail. Once he'd made certain his escape hadn't been noticed, he found a taxi. He asked to be taken to a downtown hotel.

After getting a hotel room under a false identity, Price called Britt.

"I assume you got away," Britt stated in lieu of a greeting.

"Yes. Thank you," Price replied. Unable to contain his curiosity any longer, he asked, "How'd you know they were coming for me, and do you know why?"

As a vampire, Price could have used mental manipulation to send the humans on their way. If he hadn't had a heads up, he would have, too. Except, with getting a heads up, he had a head start, since leaving with just his go-bag meant it looked like he would be home soon.

"You know I've never asked why it looks like you aren't aging," Britt began slowly.

Price grimaced. It seemed he'd forgotten just how long he'd been known as Price Litner. He should probably have used the last bad mission to fake his death. Except, if he'd done that, his entire team would have been lost instead of only two of them.

Three since the second human he'd saved, Mick, had lost

his mind and attempted to murder their final team member, Graham, which ended up with Mick's death.

That had happened almost six months before, and Price still missed his old team. They'd been aware of his nature, and they hadn't cared. In fact, on a few occasions, a couple of them had allowed Price to feed from them when their mission hadn't allowed him access to a donor.

"And according to the military database, your file has been flagged after your last drug screening."

The sound of Britt's voice through the line pulled Price out of his thoughts.

"Damn," Price muttered. "Why?"

"An anomaly in your blood," Britt told him. "Your last blood draw put you at O-negative, and for some reason, now it's reading at O-positive."

"Gods, I can't believe I did that." Price wanted to smack himself upside the head. "Such a rookie mistake."

"Uhhhh, something you want to explain?" Britt asked. "Because I know it's not possible to change that." Scoffing, he quickly continued, "You faked your blood draw, didn't you?"

"I *always* fake my blood draw," Price admitted. With a deep sigh, he told Britt, "Otherwise, I wouldn't be accepted into the military."

"Because you're not human, right?"

Price resisted the urge to roll his eyes even as he grunted agreement.

Britt scoffed softly. "That does explain a lot. Look, you don't have to tell me what you are. I don't care," he claimed. "I judge by the behavior of a person. You know that. And you're a good man."

Smirking, Price murmured, "If we were having this conversation face to face, I would tell you."

Britt's chuckle came through the line as he stated, "Maybe someday then."

"Fair enough." Price doubted he would ever see Britt again, but he didn't say that. "Thank you for the heads up. I owe you one."

"Yeah, you do," Britt quipped. "And don't think I won't collect one day."

Okay. Maybe I'll see him again after all.

"Anytime," Price vowed.

"So, what are you going to do?"

Price opened his mouth, then closed it again.

What am I going to do?

"You know what, maybe you shouldn't tell me," Britt cut in. "Just in case they decide to ask all your friends where you might go. That way, I don't have to lie to them."

Grunting, Price nodded even though he knew Britt wouldn't be able to see it. "Fair enough." With a smile, he added, "Not like I don't think you could find me when you need that favor returned."

"Exactly," Britt replied brightly. "All right, buddy. Drop a line every now and then. Talk to you later."

With that, Britt hung up.

Blowing out a breath, Price flopped back on the bed. He stared at the ceiling, wondering just where the hell he was going to go. Without the support of a coven, he had no true place to hide and no one to shield him.

Price realized he had one chance, but it was a long shot.

After dialing a number he knew by heart, Price returned the phone to his ear.

The line rang twice before a deep voice stated, "Yes?"

Smiling a little upon hearing the brusque, wary tone, Price stated, "It's good to hear your voice, Graham."

Graham's attitude immediately warmed. "Price! Hey, man. How's military life treating you?"

"Not well," Price admitted.

"They didn't find out, did they?"

Price clicked his tongue once before admitting, "They definitely know something is up with me. I had a visit from the military police today."

"Fuck," Graham growled. "What do you need from me?"

Unable to help himself, Price felt the corners of his lips curve up. "I don't know if you can help," he told him. "But I'm hopeful." After a heartbeat of hesitation, Price admitted, "You know I don't have a coven to shield me. Is there somewhere near you that I can lie low?"

"Of course. Come here," Graham immediately replied. "The pod will protect you."

Scoffing softly, Price told him, "You can't promise that, Graham. You'd need the alpha's permission."

As much as Price wished he could take Graham at his word, he knew better. The paranormal world worked a little differently than the human one. Graham had bonded with a shifter that shared his spirit with a great white shark named Eban. Shifters could turn into their animal at will and were completely cognizant while in that form.

For the first time ever, Price wished he had that ability rather than being a vampire. He could turn into his animal and hide somewhere for a few decades until he was no longer wanted by the military . . . or until he was presumed dead. Being wanted by the military, Price assumed they would be on the lookout for that sort of ploy.

Graham snorted derisively. "Man, Eban thinks he owes you a life-debt for saving me before we met," he told him with a chuckle, referring to his shifter partner. "And I'd already extended an invitation for you to visit. Remember?"

"Visiting with the intent to hide and figure out a new identity is different than a visit to say hello," Price told him. Still, he couldn't help having a little hope. A life-debt to a shifter was damn important. "How about I come up and meet with your alpha first thing so I can explain the situation."

"We'll do it your way, Price, but Alpha Kaiser will agree with me," Graham stated confidently. "When should we expect you?"

Price prayed to whatever gods cared to listen that it would play out as Graham predicted. "Thank you, Graham." After a quick distance calculation, he told him, "It'll take me about seven hours to jog that distance while avoiding detection."

"Fuck that," Graham grumbled. "Where are you? I'll come get you."

Price only hesitated a second before he told his ex-team member where he was holed up.

"Dare, are you busy?"

Turning away from where he'd just finished stocking the security office's shelves with coffee, sugar, and other basics to face Alpha Kaiser, Dare Winterwall grinned at the fellow shifter and leader of their pod. "Was just thinking about scouting the park for a one-night stand," he told him, not at all abashed to admit he was thinking about getting laid. "But that can wait. What's up?"

Dare had lived for nearly a century in his giant octopus form, never feeling safe on land. When Kaiser had tracked him down and had shared his vision of building *World of Aquatica* — a marine park utilizing aquatic shifters — he'd been flattered to be offered an enforcer position. Even after being mostly human for over a decade, he was still making up for lost time.

"Graham and Eban have gone to fetch Graham's vampire friend, Price Litner," Kaiser told him, crossing his arms over his chest. His eyes narrowed, and his brows drew together. Leaning a hip against the counter, Kaiser added, "I guess he's run into an issue, and he's running from the military."

"Ah, damn." Dare shook his head. "So is he coming here to

hide, then? I know Eban feels a bit beholden to him considering Price saved Graham's life before they even met."

Kaiser nodded. "He is, although I think he's coming to see if he's going to be accepted by me." Easing his features into a smirk, he told him, "As long as he's truthful with me, I don't have an issue with him hiding out here for however long he needs."

"Truthful?" Dare asked curiously. "About what?"

"Why he's not part of a coven." With a shrug, Kaiser lowered his arms and pushed away from the counter. "When I first learned of Eban's feelings about how Price saved Graham, I asked Master Bercham to inquire about him from the council. He was labeled rogue almost a hundred and fifty years ago, and I want to know why."

Dare hummed as he began following Kaiser out of the security office. "Makes sense."

Master Aldor Bercham led a coven based south of Sacramento. They'd always had a good working relationship with the coven. Once or twice, they'd even utilized a vampire's ability to alter a human's mind when they'd seen or learned something they shouldn't.

"Has Price been living near Master Bercham's territory?" Dare asked curiously. He waved at Rawlins, a shifter manning their security office's front desk. "Sorry, Rawlins." Winking, Dare tipped his chin toward their alpha. "I don't think I'll make it to the bar tonight. Duty calls."

Rawlins sighed as he nodded. "Yeah, figured as much when I saw you come in, Alpha Kaiser."

Kaiser chuckled softly. "Maybe Gracin or Saul would accompany you," he offered, referring to a couple of other single shifters. "I bet they would enjoy a night out."

Grinning, Rawlins nodded. "Good idea, Alpha."

Stepping out of the office, Dare felt the warm spring air

wrapping around him. He loved that it had once again become warm enough to work in polo shirts. The soft short-sleeved fabric showcased his massive muscles, which always made it easy to attract a willing bed-warmer for the night. With so many humans coming and going through the park, Dare never had any trouble finding someone interested in a little fun between the sheets.

When a blond-haired human gave him the once-over and a flirty smile, Dare winked back at him.

Too bad I can't stop to talk to him. Get his name and number.

"You're already thinking about fucking that human," Kaiser murmured, his voice soft enough for Dare's sensitive shifter hearing to pick up, but it wouldn't carry to the humans around them. "Why don't you get his number? We still have thirty minutes before I expect Eban to return."

While Dare appreciated his alpha's offer, he shook his head and picked up his pace. "Naw. I don't want to make a promise to some guy if this takes longer than you think." Seeing Kaiser arch one black brow, Dare realized how that sounded. "Uh, not that I'm second-guessing you."

Kaiser snorted and grinned. "Of course not."

Picking up their pace, they made their way to a golf cart parked around the corner from the office. Dare climbed onto the passenger seat, tucking his long legs a little awkwardly. At six-foot-six, he didn't fit in the vehicle really well, so he appreciated that he wasn't driving.

Dare enjoyed watching the scenery as they headed out of the park, driving along the windy paved trail that led to the complex of apartments and condos. Many of the employees working at the park were shifters, so Kaiser had designed homes for them just north of the park. An elevator to a massive underground grotto was housed in the largest building, and any of the shifters could utilize it. They also owned a couple of private beaches in that direction, too.

"Ah, looks like they arrived early," Kaiser commented as

he pointed toward Eban's parked truck. "Must not have hit much traffic."

"Or Eban speeded," Dare tossed out his own idea.

Kaiser chuckled as he nodded and parked.

Following Kaiser into the building, Dare noticed an intriguing scent. He cocked his head and inhaled deeply. "Huh." His blood heated and flooded south. "Do you smell that?"

Glancing his way, Kaiser nodded. "Sure. I smell that a vampire has passed by here recently."

"No, not that." Dare shook his head. "I mean . . ." After inhaling again, he couldn't fight the arousal surging through him. "Oh!"

Realization hit.

"Oh, what?" Kaiser asked as he opened the door to a room he used as his office. Holding it open, he allowed Dare to pass. Evidently, Kaiser noticed the arousal in Dare's scent. "Something you want to share with the class?"

Dare came to a stop a few feet inside and stared at the stranger standing on the other side of the room. The vampire was wiry and toned and stood around six-foot-one. His nape-length, pale-blond hair had been slicked back from his face, accentuating his high-cheek-boned features.

"You're my mate," Dare declared, in awe of the gorgeous male that Fate had deemed his.

Upon hearing Dare's voice, Price snapped his focus to him, and his pale-blue eyes widened. His lips parted, but he didn't speak.

Eban slapped Price on the shoulder, and amusement filled his tone. "Congrats, Price. Seems you're no longer rogue. Welcome to the pod."

Dare grinned widely as he continued to admire his mate. "Hell, yeah. No more one-night stands."

CHAPTER TWO

Price couldn't help it. He growled softly as he stalked toward the hulking black male who'd just blurted out the dumbest thing in history. His scent gave him away as a shifter of some kind, so why the hell would he talk about past fucks in front of him?

While, as a vampire, Price didn't confirm his beloved—the same as a mate to a shifter—until he'd tasted the other person's blood, he would never discuss other sexual partners in front of his other half. Paranormals were extremely possessive, after all.

Even as Price recognized the shifter's surprised expression, he grabbed the much larger male and pressed him against the nearest wall. Pushing his body against the other man's, he growled, "You would dare to speak of other lovers to your unclaimed mate?"

Price grabbed the man's thick, dark-skinned wrists and slapped them against the wall on either side of his head. Tipping his head a little, he placed his nose against the shifter's neck and inhaled. Relishing the iron-rich, masculine scent of his soon-to-be lover, Price felt his mouth water.

"Th-That's not what I meant," the huge male rumbled, his breath hitching.

Reveling in the fact that the shifter allowed him to manhandle him, Price nuzzled and licked over the bulge of his neck tendon. He wanted a taste so damn badly. Except, right then, someone cleared their throat.

Right. Not alone. Definitely my beloved . . . I think.

Needing to confirm, even with the audience, Price scraped his fang over the skin along his neck tendon just hard enough to pierce his skin. He heard the guy's gasp and felt the way he shuddered in his hold. Then the shifter pulled his hands free only to latch them onto Price's hips, holding him tight against him, and rocked his hips.

The taste of the shifter's blood, even the small bead that it was, exploded across Price's taste buds. He latched his lips onto the tiny mark he'd made and sucked. His fangs ached with his need to bury them deep into the male's flesh.

The sound of someone — maybe the same someone — clearing his throat even louder helped Price resist. He snapped his head up and peered at the man he'd practically mauled. From the heavy-lidded eyes and the wide grin the guy sported, Price knew he hadn't minded one bit.

"Well, Dare," that same deep voice began dryly, although there was a tinge of mirth coloring it. "Would you like to introduce me to your mate?"

Amusement filling him as Price recalled his words, he eyed the massive black man allowing him to all but maul him . . . and with a smile on his face. "Dare?"

"Dare Winterwall," he replied. With a wink and a squeeze of his hands on Price's hips, he added, "And I'm so damn happy to meet you." Then he appeared to sober a little. "And I didn't mean to talk about past lovers. I was just so fucking happy to finally have someone of my own that my brain didn't catch up with my mouth."

Price nodded, understanding completely. "And I suppose my instincts ran away with me before common sense prevailed." Resting his hands on Dare's wide shoulders, he massaged lightly as he stared into the eyes of his much larger beloved. "I appreciate that none of your people thought I was attacking you."

"Dare is one of my most capable enforcers," the man who'd

entered the room with Dare commented. "He could easily have stopped you should he have wished."

"An enforcer," Price repeated softly. "Impressive."

"Thank you." Dare scented of pleasure at hearing Price's quiet praise. "And this is Alpha Kaiser Roush, as you probably guessed."

Price had suspected, but he hadn't wanted to make any assumptions. That had only gotten him into trouble in the past. He did his best to learn from his mistakes.

Realizing the alpha was waiting to be acknowledged, Price peeled his hands off of Dare. He took a step away from his beloved and tipped his head in deference as he held out his hand. "Thank you for allowing me this meeting on such short notice."

Kaiser took his hand while touching the back of his neck with the other. After giving it the lightest of squeezes, he released him and stepped back. "It's good to finally meet you, Price," Kaiser told him. "Even better now that I know you're Dare's mate." Then he waved toward a small sofa to the left. "Please, have a seat. We have much to discuss."

Price knew an order when he heard it, and he quickly obeyed. To his pleasure, after he'd settled on one side of the sofa, Dare sat next to him. His beloved even reached over and took his hand, threading their fingers together.

Smiling at Dare, Price squeezed their twined digits. "I like this," he admitted in a hushed voice. "A little surprised you're the touchy-feely sort."

Dare shrugged his massive shoulders and waggled his eyebrows. "I bet there's a lot of things about each other that will surprise us, but we'll figure it all out."

After nodding once more, Price turned his attention to Alpha Kaiser, who'd settled in a comfortable-looking chair to his right. At some point, Eban had poured a round of drinks. There were tumblers full of something amber on the coffee table before him, and Kaiser held one in his hand.

Reaching out with his free hand, Dare snagged one, which he held out to Price. "You okay with whiskey?" he asked. "We have a stocked bar in here if you want something else."

Taking the tumbler, Price told him, "Whiskey is fine. Thank you."

Then he took a small sip. As the smooth liquid flowed over his taste buds, he realized it was a very expensive brand. He enjoyed another appreciative sip.

Dare flashed another smile before grabbing the second one for himself.

Kaiser lowered the glass he'd just been drinking from and smirked at him. His deep green eyes twinkled with amusement as he stated, "And now, the inquisition begins."

Price had expected as much. "Yes, Alpha."

Dare barely managed to withhold his growl of displeasure. He'd known why they were meeting Price, and they needed the information. He just wished he was learning about his mate and his past in private. Then Dare could have related the relevant bits to his alpha later.

Too bad the meeting had already been planned.

"Relax, Dare," Kaiser rumbled, obviously catching on to his unease. "I won't ask anything too intrusive, but you know we need to be aware of what could be coming our way." His eyes narrowed, the mirth disappearing. "Knowledge is power."

"Yes, Alpha," Dare immediately replied. "Meeting my mate has affected me in a way I hadn't realized."

"Understandable," Eban commented from where he'd settled beside Graham. "When we picked up Price, even though I knew there wasn't anything between them, just the memory of my mate telling me he'd fed Price his blood made me want to deck him." As Eban finished, he grinned wickedly.

Dare gave in to the need to growl. "You fed from Graham?" he demanded, frowning at Price.

"Oh, good grief," Graham grumbled. "It wasn't like there was anything between us," he claimed, shaking his head as he scowled at Eban. "And don't cause trouble, Eban, or you're sleeping on the couch."

Eban's eyes widened as a stricken expression crossed his features. "No, babe," he cried. "That wasn't what I was trying to do."

Price squeezed Dare's hand, drawing his focus back to him. "Graham is right. He fed me his blood twice. Both were times when a mission went awry, and I couldn't get somewhere to find a donor." His expression remained serious as he added, "There was nothing sexual about it."

Dare decided the best thing for everyone would be to change the subject. It wasn't like he was some innocent, so he knew his jealousy was silly. Hell, he'd just been admiring a human in the marine park.

I have no room to judge.

"Sorry, my mate," Dare forced out, even if his voice was a little gruffer than normal. "These urges are hitting fast, huh?"

Nodding, Price agreed. Turning to Alpha Kaiser, his mate stated, "I'm aware you'll need to know what could be coming your way by me being here, and I'm happy to tell you everything I can." Grimacing, he admitted, "Which, unfortunately, isn't much."

Alpha Kaiser tipped his chin in a slight nod. "What happened that sent you running? Who are you running from?"

Sighing, Price relaxed against the sofa. He even pressed his shoulder against Dare's arm, as if seeking comfort. Dare wasn't certain if the vampire knew he did it, but he appreciated it just the same, pressing back against him a little in silent support.

"The military," Price revealed. "A friend tipped me off a

few minutes before military police showed up at my door."

"Damn," Graham muttered. "What do they want you for?"

Evidently, Price hadn't revealed everything to his buddy on the drive in.

"Being a vampire, I can't very well allow blood donations during physicals or drug screenings," Price told them. "So I take some from a human the day before, put whatever technician is supposed to draw my blood in a trance, and make him believe the human's blood is mine."

"Let me guess," Kaiser commented drolly. "Something went wrong. Did you run into a technician you couldn't trance?"

Price shook his head, embarrassment flooding his scent as his pale cheeks took on a slightly pinkish hue. "I'd just returned from a mission and was ordered to take a random drug test. I didn't have time to be as discerning as I usually am when preparing for these things." With a sigh, he admitted, "The guy I grabbed ended up having O-positive blood instead of the O-negative I've always used in the past."

"Oh, fuck," Graham muttered. "That'll raise a flag."

"Exactly," Price agreed. "I suppose I could have found a way around it, but I've been Price Litner for so long, it'll be tough to make them believe I'm only thirty-eight for much longer." Grimacing, Price added, "Britt, my friend who tipped me off, has already noticed."

"Does he know what you are?" Kaiser asked, narrowing his eyes.

"He knows I'm not human," Price admitted. Perhaps guessing that Kaiser would consider the human's knowledge a danger, Dare's vampire quickly lifted his tumbler and stated, "He doesn't know specifics, but if he were here, I'd tell him. I trust him with my life."

"You must if you fled due to his warning," Dare pointed out. Wanting to know more about his mate's desires, he asked, "Do you want this fixed so you can return to the military?"

Please say no.

Price smirked as he shook his head. "No. Even if I hadn't met you" — he lifted their twined fingers and pressed a kiss to Dare's knuckles — "I would still be planning to move on."

"Then we make you look like you've fled another direction," Kaiser stated, relaxing in his seat. He rested his left ankle over his right knee and balanced his tumbler on his leg. "I'll have Ovram set up a false trail which will lead the military east into the mountains."

"Thank you," Price replied, although his eyebrows furrowed. "Even still, you may end up with military police here to question Graham. He's the only surviving member of my old unit and an obvious person of interest."

"He's right," Graham confirmed with a smirk. "And I'll be ready."

Price smiled at Graham, clearly thankful.

"Soooo," Kaiser mused. "That brings us to the second matter we need to discuss."

Sighing with resignation, Price nodded. "Right. My rogue status."

"Indeed," Kaiser confirmed. Arching one brow, he stared critically at Price, "You don't seem out of control, so what happened?"

Dare opened his mouth, ready to defend his mate, but Price squeezed his hand and smiled at him. "Graham already knows, and this is your inner circle," his mate told him. "They have a right to know."

Snapping his mouth shut, Dare nodded. "Okay."

"Just over a hundred and fifty years ago, I was part of a coven in Tennessee," Price began before taking a sip of his whiskey. "It was run by a powerful master who had the bad habit of allowing his dick to do the thinking."

Sneering, Dare interjected, "Did you refuse him, and that's

why he kicked you out?"

Price scoffed and shook his head. "Oh, no. I wasn't his type," he revealed. "He was straight as an arrow."

"Then?" Kaiser pressed.

Narrowing his eyes, Price stared into his drink. "His favorite donor, a woman named Wisteria, decided she wanted to sleep with me." He lifted his focus and peered at Kaiser. "I knew what a bad idea that was, considering she was the master's, so I declined"—after a second of hesitation, Price added—"in a way I thought was gracious and flattering."

"Didn't work, did it?" Graham muttered, relaxing against Eban's side. "What'd she do?"

Price shook his head. "No, it didn't work. She kept asking, and I kept coming up with polite ways of saying no." After gulping the last of his whiskey, he placed the tumbler on the coffee table. With his free hand, Price rubbed his thigh in agitation. "She cornered me in the hallway one evening after supper. I thought she planned to throw herself at me again, but she didn't." He lifted his hand and rubbed it across his cheek as his expression turned a little vacant. "Wisteria slapped me across the face and declared that she would never sleep with me and to stop asking. To say I was shocked was an understatement, and I just stood there like an imbecile as she turned and fled down the hall . . . right into Master Drawman's arms."

"Oh, fuck," Dare mumbled. "I know where this is going."

"We all know," Eban grumbled, shaking his head. "He didn't even question her, did he? Or you. Just banished you on the spot."

Price nodded. "I tried to explain, to counter what it had looked like. I know he could scent my truthfulness. The second was right there, and he looked at the master as if he had two heads."

"You were banished and labeled rogue for the mistreatment of donors," Alpha Kaiser stated.

Scenting of surprise, Price murmured, "Yes, I was. How did you know the reason?"

Kaiser smiled warmly at him. "I'm on good terms with the nearby coven, and I looked into you," he told him, obviously completely comfortable with his actions.

Dare knew his alpha took the care and safety of those under him seriously—not only the shifters under his care, but the humans, too—both mates and employees.

That meant researching people, and Kaiser had no qualms doing it.

"Anyway, I left. For the first year, I tried to find a place in a new coven, but no one would risk taking me in," Price continued as if he needed to get it all out of the way. "Almost five decades later, I heard the second had taken over the coven less than two years after I was banished." Scoffing, Price finished, "It's never a good thing to have a master who allows himself to be led around by his dick by a lying donor."

"Indeed it is not," Kaiser confirmed. Then he smiled and stated, "You have a place here in my pod, if you want it. I'd prefer it, actually, since I don't want to lose Dare."

Dare almost held his breath as he waited for Price's response.

Price smiled at Kaiser. "Thank you, Alpha Kaiser. I'd like that."

The alpha rose, signaling the end of the meeting. "I'm going to talk to Ovram now. I'll keep you posted on developments with the military." Then he left the room.

After downing the last of his drink, Dare popped to his feet, tugging Price with him. He needed to get his mate alone and in his space.

Preferably naked.

"Come on," Dare urged, leading the way out of the office. To his pleasure, Price didn't resist.

CHAPTER THREE

Price would have laughed at the eagerness Dare displayed, but he didn't think the huge shifter would appreciate that. Instead, he marveled at the changes barreling into his life in such a short time. He'd essentially lost his job, found a new home, a new pod, and his beloved.

Just damn.

Dare stopped at an elevator and pressed a button. Then he turned and dropped Price's hand. Before he could feel the loss, Dare wrapped both arms around him and pulled him flush to his body.

"Please tell me that, when we get to my condo, I can claim you," Dare rumbled, dipping his head until his lips were only an inch away from Price's. "You're my mate, and I wish to bind you to me in every way possible."

Price grinned up at Dare, rubbing his palms over his broad torso. "I'm a vampire, Dare. I feel the pull the same as you do."

"Then we'll talk after we fuck," Dare declared with a roguish grin. "Pillow talk while naked, maybe with a glass of wine or beer. After that, we'll explore each other's bodies all over again."

The door dinged and opened, and Dare urged Price backward into the car. As soon as the doors closed and his beloved had pushed the button for the tenth floor, his new and forever lover crowded him into the corner.

Before Dare could capture his lips — something Price really wanted him to do — he told his shifter, "You know that means

I intend to fuck you, too."

Dare grinned broadly as he waggled his eyebrows. "I sure hope so . . . and more." Pressing his lips to Price's, he flicked out his tongue and swiped it over his bottom lip.

Price opened instantly, welcoming Dare's advances. As he clung to his big shifter's wide shoulders, he couldn't recall the last time he'd been the smaller in a pairing. Accepting Dare's tongue into his mouth, feeling him tease along his fangs, knowing he didn't have to hide them from his partner, Price realized it didn't matter. He didn't care.

All that mattered was the shifter rubbing his hands over his body, sliding them under his shirt, and setting fire to the skin of his back. When Dare teased his tongue down one fang then up the other, a moan of pure bliss erupted from Price's throat. His gut clenched as his groin tightened, and his cock throbbed in time with his pounding heartbeats.

"Gods, it's like *Love Boat* around here. No wonder Rawlins called me when you bailed," a melodious tenor griped. "You already found a bootie call. Couldn't make it to your room, Dare?"

Dare lifted his head and glared over his shoulder at whoever had interrupted.

Price didn't know when the elevator had stopped or when the doors had opened, but a lithe, six-foot-one, black-haired man stood in the doorway. He had his arms crossed and a smirk on his face. His painted-on jeans and form-fitting polo told Price the man was obviously heading out for an evening of . . . fun.

"Watch your mouth, Gracin," Dare snarled, telling Price the shifter's name. "Don't talk about my mate that way."

"Your mate?" Gracin sounded incredulous. His brown eyes were wide as he continued, "Since when?"

"Since right now," Dare countered, the acrid scent of his anger beginning to fill the elevator. "Apologize. Now!"

Price rubbed up and down Dare's chest, hoping to soothe his angry beloved.

Fortunately, the clearly shocked Gracin pulled his head out of his ass. He dipped his head a bit in obvious deference, telling Price the man wasn't a higher ranking enforcer than Dare. "I'm so sorry, Dare. I was just shocked." He smiled as he focused on Price. "And my apologies to you, too, Dare's mate. I'm not usually such an asshole. Just, um—" Gracin looked away, a pained expression crossing his face.

The scent of Dare's ire immediately eased as the tension drained from his body. "What's wrong, Gray?" he asked. Then he waved a hand at the unhappy shifter. "This is Gracin, by the way. He's a genius at marketing. Gracin, this is Price, my mate."

"Nice to meet you," Gracin offered with a half-hearted wave. Then he shoved his hands into his pockets. "Just didn't get a marketing deal I'd been working on. I thought it was in the bag, but I got a call from the investor this afternoon, and they've changed their minds."

"That sucks," Dare consoled. "It sounds like a night out to forget your troubles is just what you need then."

Gracin sighed deeply as he nodded. "Yeah. Hope I can get in the mood and don't bring down Rawlins and Saul."

Dare smiled as he told him, "If anyone can pull you out of your funk, Rawlins can."

As Dare spoke, he guided Price from the elevator, allowing Gracin to move inside.

Nodding again, Gracin hit a button. "Hope so." Then his smile turned more genuine. "Congratulations, guys." As the door closed, Gracin waggled his eyebrows and teased, "Have a great night!"

"Oh, we will," Dare replied gruffly, his tone full of innuendo. Then Gracin was gone, and Dare wrapped his arm around Price's waist. "Come on." As they strode down the hallway, Dare asked, "Am I pushing you, Price? I don't mean to. I just—"

Price reached up and touched his forefinger to Dare's lips, making his words stall. "I'm a vampire, Dare," he reminded him. "I feel the exact same pull as you do." Seeing that Dare still looked a little unsure, Price realized the issue. "Your pod-members have only found human mates, haven't they?"

Dare nodded as he opened the door they'd stopped in front of. "Yeah."

"And they take a little time. Some convincing," Price stated, understanding.

"Right."

Price placed his hand on Dare's back and pushed lightly, urging his beloved into the room. "I'm a vampire, not a human," Price reminded again. "I don't have that hang-up. This is the way of paranormals. We meet the other half of our soul. We bond. After that, we figure out how to make our lives work together." Closing the door behind them, Price gripped Dare's wrist, rubbing the pulse point there, pleased to feel it racing beneath his touch. "Can you handle that, Dare?"

Dare's heated smile cleared all of Price's concerns. "Hell yeah, I can."

"Then show me to your bedroom, my beloved," Price crooned huskily as he raked his gaze over the gorgeous specimen of maleness that was his shifter. "Because I don't intend for our first time to be against a wall." Then Price pinned his beloved with a hungry look. "Not that I wouldn't want to explore that another time."

Groaning, his gray eyes stormy with need, Dare twisted his hand so he was gripping Price's wrist, too. "This way." Then he began tugging, leading him through the suite.

Price barely paid attention to the décor until he reached the bedroom. The bed was . . . massive—probably a custom. As he watched Dare strip his polo shirt from his huge torso, the size of the furniture made sense.

"If you want to be able to wear those clothes again," Dare began, dropping his shirt on the floor and reaching for the fly of his jeans. "You'd better start stripping."

"As sexy as I find that, I only have one other pair," Price admitted as he grabbed his t-shirt's hem and started tugging it over his head.

Even with the fabric around his ears, Price heard Dare ask, "Really?"

"Really," Price confirmed as he pulled free of his shirt. His mouth went dry at the stunning male before him. "Oh, fuck me."

Dare's six-foot-six frame was beautifully proportioned. His shoulders were wide, and his body and limbs were thickly muscled. His torso tapered to a trim waist, and he sported an eight-pack. The vee at his hips pointed like an arrow to the huge erection jutting from his groin.

"Oh, I definitely intend to do that," Dare claimed, palming his hefty piece of meat. "Over and over and over again." His grin turned feral as he lifted his other hand. "After you fuck and claim me, my mate, and while you do that, I'm going to open you up." Dare's expression sobered. "I know I'm big. I'll never do anything to hurt you."

Price nodded slowly, unable to tear his gaze away from Dare's rod. "You are huge. Twelve inches?" he guessed.

"Yep." Dare sounded smug. "That's why I'll get you ready while you're distracted."

Finally pulling his attention from Dare's beautiful tool, Price cocked his head. "How do you plan to do that?"

As Price watched, Dare's hand and arm, up to his elbow, changed. It lengthened and split, turning into . . . tentacles.

Dread ripped through Price's system as he spotted those gray appendages, and he stumbled backward. In a flash, he had the bed between them.

"What the fuck?" Price shrieked, unable to control his response as every hint of arousal drained from his system.

What the fuck seemed to sum it up nicely.

Dare froze as he tried to figure out what the hell had just happened. Glancing at his hand, he frowned as he returned his appendage to an arm and fingers. He focused again on Price, relieved to see that, while he still appeared pale and was breathing heavily, his eyes were no longer wide with terror ... and that same scent was beginning to ease—very slowly.

Holding his hands, palms up and out, Dare asked, "Price? Please talk to me, my mate. What did I do wrong?"

He wanted to move across the room and wrap him in his arms, but he worried how his clearly traumatized mate would respond.

What the hell happened to my vampire?

"Y-Your arm," Price stuttered. "W-What was, um"—he finally managed to meet Dare's gaze—"going on with your arm?"

"You know I'm a shifter, Price," Dare began slowly. Upon getting a confused-looking nod from Price, he continued, "I was shifting part of my arm, so I could show you how I was going to open up your ass while you fucked me." With an encouraging smile, Dare added, "You'll love it. I promise. I'd never hurt you. Remember?"

Dare knew it didn't sound nearly as sexy as how it felt. He should know. He'd pleasured himself with his tentacles more times than he could count. Dare knew just how to move his appendage without ever causing harm with his suckers.

"Y-Your animal?" Price whispered, the scent of his trepidation returning. "W-W-What animal?"

Dare heard his octopus low softly in his mind, and he shared his beast's worry. His mate was a vampire. Why was

24

he so worried about his animal? Surely Price knew that Dare was completely cognizant while in animal form.

Right?

"Price, I share my spirit with a giant octopus," Dare told him slowly. To his disappointment, he saw the little blood that had returned to Price's face drain away. "My mate." Unable to help himself, Dare took a step forward, but he stopped when he saw the tension in his mate's body intensify. "My mate, why does this upset you? You knew I was a shifter, and you were okay with it." Trying to reason it out, Dare added, "Or is seeing it different than knowing, even in theory?"

Price's narrow torso expanded as he took a deep breath, then relaxed as he exhaled. He did that two more times, telling Dare he was trying to calm himself.

As much as it pained him, Dare knew Price needed a little space. Staying on his side of his massive, custom-sized bed, he walked slowly toward the headboard. Dare moved a pillow against the dark wood, then sat down cross-legged, his back leaning on it . . . and he waited.

Fortunately, it didn't take too long.

"Please don't shift again, Dare," Price whispered roughly. He glanced into Dare's eyes, then away again, before saying, "I know you won't hurt me in animal form, so please give me a chance to explain why."

"Fair enough," Dare replied softly, doing his best to keep his voice kind, understanding even. Although, inside, he was doing everything he could to reassure his animal. His beast was a part of him. If his mate was rejecting half of him, the mating could never turn out well.

As if Price could read his mind—hell, eventually, as a vampire, assuming they bonded, the vampire would be able to read certain thoughts—he whispered, "I'm not rejecting you, your animal, or our bond. This is just . . . an unexpected development."

Dare nodded again, even though he had no idea what he

was agreeing to. "Okay."

Price rested his hands on his hips and tipped his head back. For a few seconds, he stared at the ceiling, but his expression remained vacant. After a moment, Price focused on Dare again and offered a tremulous smile.

"The information I'm about to tell you is classified," Price told him as he moved slowly to the head of his side of the bed. "You can't repeat it."

Nodding, Dare guessed, "You're about to tell me about one of your missions."

"I am," Price confirmed.

To Dare's relief—and pleasure—Price eased onto the bed. His vampire faced him, resting on his left butt cheek and hand with his legs cocked to the right. He placed his right arm on his upturned leg.

"Anything you tell me will remain between us," Dare told his mate. Then, after a second of hesitation, he added, "Unless it's something that my alpha must know to protect the pod."

"Fair enough," Price replied softly. Then, after blowing out a soft breath, he met Dare's gaze and told him, "This was back when I still worked with Graham and our team."

Dare nodded again, understanding.

"We were sent to a coastal town in northern Japan," Price told him. "We were to take out the leaders of a human trafficking ring."

Grimacing, Dare hated to think of anyone forced into servitude of any kind. Seeing the lines of tension on Price's face, he gave in to instinct, reached out, and rested his hand over his mate's. For a second, Price remained frozen under his touch. Then his vampire smiled, flipped his hand over, and twined their fingers.

"Our information was faulty, and we walked into an ambush," Price stated, shaking his head. He furrowed his brows, and his body tensed. "I allowed myself to be captured, so everyone else could escape, thinking I could use my trancing abilities to get away." Price shook his head. "They used a tranquilizer on me, and while it didn't knock me out, it did sedate me enough to where I couldn't drum up enough concentration to manipulate everyone in the room."

"You were tortured," Dare whispered, hating to think of his mate in any kind of danger, let alone being purposefully injured for information.

"Right." Price met and held his gaze. "They inserted a fish up my rectum and submerged most of my body in a tank full of octopi." A shudder went through him as he finished, "And let me tell you, alien probing has nothing on a hungry octopus trying to fish out its next meal."

Dare cringed, fighting back his queasiness. "I-I'm so sorry, my mate."

Price sighed deeply as he squeezed Dare's hand. "It's not your fault." Then his cheeks pinked a little as his gaze slid to the dark-blue comforter on the bed. "But it did leave me with a fear of . . . tentacles."

Even as Dare completely understood how that could happen, he couldn't help but mutter, "Shit."

CHAPTER FOUR

Price hadn't meant to put a damper on their evening, but he hadn't been able to control his freak-out, either. Seeing the gray appendages coming from Dare's arm had taken him back in time so completely, he'd been able to think of only one thing—escape. He'd had to put as much distance between himself and the tentacles as he could.

"I'm sorry that happened to you, Price," Dare rumbled softly, squeezing his fingers in slow rhythmic pulses. "But you know, as a shifter, our animal is part of us." His deep gray eyes held a wealth of concern as he continued, "Even when in animal form, I'll always know who you are, what you mean to us."

Shifting his weight, Price lifted his other hand and placed it over Dare's. He hated that he'd put that expression on the huge, confident black man's face—a mixture of worry and trepidation. As much as he wished he could remove it by saying he would get over it, he couldn't lie to him.

"I do know that, Dare. Truly," Price told him. "But you should also know that some fears aren't rational."

Dare sighed deeply even as he nodded. "Of course." Meeting his gaze, he asked, "Is there anything I can do to reassure you? To . . . help you?"

Price opened his mouth to respond but closed it just as quickly. Unable to meet Dare's hopeful gaze, he whispered, "Please don't shift around me, yet."

Even in his peripheral vision, Price spotted the pained expression that flitted so swiftly across Dare's features—there

28

and gone. Then his beloved cleared his throat and nodded. "Yes, my mate."

Hearing Dare's soft acceptance should have reassured Price. Instead, it felt like a punch to the gut. He scented his beloved's disappointment, his sadness, but he wasn't sure how to fix it.

Still, Price had to try.

Price leaned forward, reached out, and cradled Dare's jaw. "I've never had a reason to try to overcome this before now, Dare," he murmured with a squeeze to their twined fingers. "Don't give up on me. We can get through this." Forcing himself to continue, Price couldn't help the way his voice hitched. "I-I'll meet your o-octopus soon enough, once I've had a little time to accept this. Okay?"

Gods, a vampire enforcer turned warrior, soldier, and Navy SEAL brought low by tentacled creatures.

Dare met his gaze squarely, and a small smile played around the corners of his thick lips. "We're paranormals. Soul-mates." His smile widened a little. "We'll get through this . . . no matter what." Nuzzling into Price's touch, Dare whispered, "While I know my octopus won't be able to wait forever, if it gets to the point where I can't keep him at bay around you, we'll go to the alpha for help."

Price nodded, grateful for his beloved's understanding. "Thank you."

Cocking his head, Dare narrowed his eyes. He turned his head and kissed Price's palm even as he continued to hold his gaze. Then he grinned widely as he yanked on their combined hands.

In the next instant, Price found himself sprawled face-down on the bed. Then he was flipped to his back. Staring up in surprise, he peered into Dare's grinning features.

Dare's smile faded to be replaced by a serious expression. "Did you really think I would put off claiming you because of one little hiccup?"

Price smiled sadly at his beloved. "Dare, we both know this isn't a *little* hiccup."

Shrugging one massive shoulder, Dare told him, "Maybe it's not, but that's not going to stop me from making you mine, Price." His eyes narrowed. "You *are* mine, and Fate wouldn't have paired us if we couldn't make a go of it. This is just a bump in the road, and we'll get past it."

As Price took in Dare's confident expression and heard his firm tone, his own trepidation began to fade. He found his own lips curving into a small smile. Relaxing under his beloved's hold, he lifted his arms and began rubbing over the big shifter's pectorals.

"Thank you for the vote of confidence," Price whispered. He wished he had as much faith in himself as his beloved did, but he kept those thoughts firmly to himself. "Thank you for not changing your mind."

"I *have* changed my mind," Dare replied, much to Price's surprise. Then he swept his gaze over Price's half-naked frame. "But not about bonding with you."

Confused, Price paused in rubbing his palms over every inch of Dare's smooth dark skin that he could reach. "What do you mean?"

Dare growled softly as he reached down and unsnapped the button of Price's jeans. "For a few seconds there, I thought you were rejecting me and my animal," he admitted, frowning. "I need to claim you now, so I'm going to suck your dick, open up your ass, and sink deep inside you." Dare met Price's gaze with a serious look and finished, "I'm going to pour my seed into your ass and sink my teeth into your neck, bonding us for all time."

Price opened his mouth, then closed it just as quickly. His heart rate spiked in his chest—from arousal instead of fear—and he grinned.

"Nothing would make me happier," Price whispered, still

all for bonding with his beloved. Needing to express that, he added, "Thank you for accepting me . . . bumps and all."

His expression softening, Dare replied huskily, "It's my pleasure, Price."

Then Dare dipped his head and captured Price's mouth in a kiss that scattered his thoughts and curled his toes.

Dare couldn't help it. After thinking he was being rejected because of his animal, he had to seal their bond. He needed to feel his mate beneath him, around him, to sink into his body and claim him for eternity.

As much as Dare would welcome Price's possession when the time came, he could no longer wait to be second. His animal instincts demanded that he claim the vampire. Fortunately, his mate seemed to understand.

When Dare unzipped his fly, Price lifted his hips. He quickly stripped the man of his jeans, only to get them stuck on the boots he still wore. Growling in frustration, he prepared to rend the offending fabric from his mate's calves.

"Hey," Price crooned, gripping a wrist in each hand. "Relax, my beloved. I'm not going anywhere."

Lifting his focus from the annoying clothes, Dare arched one brow as he met Price's gaze. "No," he declared. "You're not." Then Dare gave his soon-to-be lover a feral grin. "Not until you're exhausted and sweaty, and I carry you to the shower."

Price smirked up at him. "Never had anyone carry me before." Waggling his brows as he toed off his boots, he added, "Maybe I'll be carrying you instead."

Dare barked a laugh as he watched his mate finally shuck his jeans, taking his socks with them. When Price sprawled back on his elbows, stretching out before him, Dare took his time ogling the vampire, reveling in the fact that his mate was a man after his own heart. Price went commando, leaving every inch of him on display.

His legs were well defined and muscular. He had a lean, tapered waist. The neatly trimmed hairs on his groin were far fairer than his head, making them nearly white. The vampire's pale skin appeared almost milky colored, and he couldn't wait to mark it with fingernails, nips, and hickies. His light-pink nipples begged to be sucked.

Price lifted his hand and waved his fingertips in an *up here* motion.

Arching one brow, Dare offered a silent question.

"You staring at something?" Price teased.

Dare nodded, his breath catching in his throat. "Staring at the most stunning man I've ever had the privilege to see."

Snorting, Price shook his head even as he smirked at him. "I'm pretty sure every shifter feels that way about their mate." His expression sobered as he swept his gaze over Dare. "I know that's how I feel about you, my beloved."

"While you're probably right, I don't care," Dare stated. Then he spotted the way Price was sweeping his gaze over him and tilted his head. "What?"

Price grinned up at him. "There's something to the look in your eyes that tells me you don't believe me when I tell you I could carry you into the shower."

Dare rolled his eyes as he shook his head. "You're a vampire, so I know you can physically." Pinning a hungry look on his naked mate in his bed, he rumbled, "But it's getting me to agree that you'll have trouble with."

While Dare had always considered himself an easy-going guy, there was no way in hell he wanted to be carried . . . by anyone . . . even his mate. He hoped that didn't end up being a deal-breaker. If it was, Dare knew he would become extremely good at distracting his lover.

"Not a fan of being carried?" Price guessed astutely.

Holding Price's gaze, Dare admitted, "Afraid not. Hope it's not going to be an issue."

Chuckling, Price sprawled on his back and folded his arms behind his head. "Not at all. Although, I don't think you should get used to carrying me, either." He smirked as he spread his legs a little wider. "I like being on my own two feet."

"Just for the occasional play and care," Dare promised, understanding Price's point of view. His mate was a strong warrior and soldier, after all. "Now then." Dare eased between Price's legs and sprawled over him, resting his weight on his elbows on either side of his new and forever lover. "Let's set aside discussions for later."

"Yessss," Price hissed, wrapping his arms around Dare. "Where's your lube?"

Dare grinned broadly, pleased to see Price's eagerness. Leaning over, he grabbed the lube from his nightstand. Settling on his knees between his welcoming mate's, Dare popped the cap and poured a liberal dollop onto the fingers of his right hand.

After using a thumb to close the tube, Dare dropped it to the comforter. He bent forward and pressed a light kiss to Price's lips. Before giving in to the urge to delve deep into his mouth and lose himself in his mate's taste, Dare ended the kiss. He skimmed his lips along his jawline, nuzzling as he went. When Dare worked down Price's neck and his mate tipped his chin, offering more room, Dare barely resisted taking a bite right that second.

Kissing and licking down Price's body, tasting every inch of the pale flesh he was quickly becoming obsessed with, Dare used his dry hand to explore along his side, ribs, and hip. He latched onto one nipple and suckled lightly, relishing Price's soft grunt and the way he arched beneath him. Dare also appreciated his mate's hands on him, one on his head and the other on his neck. Price didn't push or demand, just touching for the connection.

When Dare began teasing his fingertip over Price's hole, a thought struck him. As much as he wished he didn't have to bring up his mate's painful past, he needed to be certain of something.

Meeting Price's gaze, Dare whispered, "I don't want to hurt you or upset you." Never did he want to do something to traumatize his mate as he'd accidentally done a few minutes before, and his mate had been violated before being rescued on a mission. "But I need to know it's okay to touch you here."

Ever-so-gently, Dare teased Price's entrance once more.

Price's expression softened, warmth filling his eyes. "It's fine, Dare," he assured. "As long as it's your fingers and not—" He winced and glanced to the side.

Moving his hand up to cradle Price's jaw, Dare urged his mate to meet his gaze again. "Never again until you ask me to," he vowed.

Seeing Price's look of relief, Dare decided he needed to replace that with pleasure. With that thought in mind, he returned his focus to his vampire's pale chest. He licked and sucked on a nipple while scraping his nails along the grooves of his abdominals. While doing that, Dare pressed a finger deep into Price's passage. The warmth clamped onto his finger, wrapping it in silky heat and causing his cock to throb in anticipation.

Can hardly wait.

As Dare began kissing his way down the center line of Price's strong, toned chest, he admired the red marks his hands and teeth were leaving on his vampire's skin. His possessive nature roared with satisfaction, and he intended to renew those marks daily. When Dare's chin bumped into Price's cock head, he nuzzled his way down it before tipping his head and licking over the flared flesh.

Price's unique flavor burst across his tongue, light with a hint of salty tang.

Dare hummed appreciatively, opened his mouth, and swallowed Price to the root.

Moaning with pleasure, Price bucked his hips.

Reaching up, Dare tweaked one of Price's nubs while sucking hard and drawing off his prick. He eased his finger mostly out of his mate's passage, then added a second as he pushed back in. His mate took it beautifully, opening to him and writhing from his ministrations.

Dare continued to work Price's body, opening him and pleasuring him, doing his best to distract from the stretch and send his lover's senses soaring.

When Dare had three fingers in Price and was preparing to add a fourth, he heard his vampire mumbling his name. He peered up the lean body he was already completely smitten with and, as he suckled his lover's crown, arched one brow in question.

Price met his gaze with dilated eyes. "G-Gonna . . . gonna . . ."

Smiling around his tasty mouthful, Dare continued to hold Price's gaze as he sucked more of his mate's erection into his mouth. He heard Price's breathing hitch, saw his jaw open, and heard his mate's lusty moan. A second later, warm cum filled his mouth, the delicious salty flavor flowing over his taste buds.

Taking complete advantage of Price being in the throes of ecstasy, Dare eased a fourth finger into his lover as he continued to suck and swallow. To his delight, he found his vampire loose and comfortable as he fucked him with his fingers. As soon as Price stopped shooting, Dare could wait no longer.

Dare released Price's prick with a soft pop and eased his digits from his body. Levering over him, he grabbed his aching shaft and used the rest of the lube on his fingers to grease his rod. Gritting his teeth at the pleasure, he quickly guided himself to Price's hole.

Touching his cock head to Price's prepared opening, Dare paused an instant. He met his mate's gaze, asking silently for permission.

Price's grin appeared a little loopy as he murmured, "Claim me, my beloved."

Only too happy to agree, Dare eased into Price. Heat and pressure surrounded his erection as he burrowed deeply into the vampire. In one lone, smooth glide, Dare buried his cock to the root.

Panting softly, trying to gather some modicum of control, Dare peered into the eyes of the man who was the other half of his soul.

"Mine," Dare whispered huskily.

Price wrapped his arms around Dare, holding him tightly. "And you're mine."

There was nothing to say after that, and Dare began to move, claiming his vampire so all the paranormal world would know to whom Price belonged.

CHAPTER FIVE

Dare set up a punishing rhythm, and Price reveled in the desire and need pouring off his beloved. He'd known his freak-out had set off his shifter's territorial and possessive instincts, but until the man had entered him, had begun to rut, he hadn't realized how much Dare had been hiding from him. Even fearing rejection, the huge man had been a kind, caring, and exquisite lover.

Price couldn't wait to return the favor.

Right then, however, all Price could do was hang on to Dare and enjoy the ride.

And gods, what a ride.

Dare's strokes were swift and forceful, filling Price over and over, rubbing his inner walls in the most delicious way. He rubbed over his prostate on each entrance and retreat. Sparks fired through Price's groin, causing his dick to stay hard and throbbing.

With the way Dare arched over him, Price's erection rubbed over his abdominals with each thrust. He clung to his beloved's big body, and his beaded nipples slipped and slid against Dare's sweaty chest. The scent of arousal, seed, and masculine sweat bathed the room in the headiest perfume.

"Want you to come for me again, mate," Dare demanded, licking and sucking on Price's neck tendon. "Want to feel you contract around my cock. Want to experience your scent on my skin. Bathe me in it."

As Dare made his demands, he reached between them and gripped Price's dick in a tight hold. He stroked him in time with his thrusts, while nailing his prostate — every move combining to send Price's senses reeling with bliss.

Price's body obeyed Dare's demand. His orgasm slammed through him, ripping a hard shudder from him. He groaned Dare's name as his cock erupted with ecstasy-inducing spurts.

Floating on the endorphins of his release, Price vaguely recognized the heat filling his passage from Dare's release. He hummed, reveling in the fact that he'd been marked internally. Then he felt Dare's teeth at his neck and knew what was to come.

Tipping his head to the side, Price murmured Dare's name in encouragement.

A spark of pain stabbed through his shoulder, but only for an instant, to quickly be replaced by heated tingles. Feeling teeth in his flesh for the first time, he absently wondered if this was how donors felt. Then Dare began to suckle on his flesh, and all thoughts fled as a fresh orgasm swamped him.

With pleasure coursing through his body, Price reveled in the sensation of being claimed. For several earth-shattering heartbeats, they stayed together like that — Dare's cock and teeth buried inside Price's body. He felt complete in a way he never could have imagined.

In too short a time, Price felt Dare ease his canines from his neck. He hummed and turned his head, catching the way his beloved licked his lips and swallowed. The pleased smile on his shifter's face gave Price a sense of satisfaction he'd never before experienced.

Rubbing his palms up Dare's neck, Price slid them over his bald head. He hadn't felt any stubble before, and he didn't then. Eventually, he would ask if it was natural, but right then, he had other things on his mind.

"That was incredible, my beloved," Price murmured, smiling up at his man. "Gonna ask you to bite me often."

Dare grinned down at him. "Heard from my buddies that

the claiming bite is orgasmic." Cocking his head, he furrowed his brows. "But you didn't bite me in return."

Price grinned, showing off his fangs. Licking one, he liked the way Dare stared at them. His nostrils even flared with his obvious interest. Even the cock in his chute remained hard.

"You really, *really* like the idea of me biting you," Price commented, his own excitement flaring anew. "You want it badly."

Nodding once, Dare admitted, "Crave it. Need you to claim me, my mate." Then his expression turned a little pensive. "Uh, while you were pretty blissed out, I stretched myself."

While Price didn't remember floating on ecstasy that long, he didn't mind his shifter's confession. "Well, well," he replied with a grin. "It would be a horrible waste not to take advantage of your actions."

Price pushed aside the thought of how Dare could have done that in favor of wrapping one of his legs around his beloved's waist. Coupled with his arms and a push from the leg planted on the comforter, he rolled them. To Price's pleasure, Dare went with the move, even as they both hissed when Dare's prick slipped free of his chute.

In seconds, Price lay sprawled over his much larger beloved. He planted his hands on either side of Dare's head even as he got his knees under him. Straddling his shifter, Price bent and placed a hard kiss on Dare's lips, taking a few seconds to dip his tongue inside his mouth. He tasted a heady mixture of Dare, seed, and blood, and the flavors immediately went to his head—his little head.

Even after three orgasms, Price's cock throbbed with the need to be buried inside his lover.

"Where's the lube?" Price demanded gruffly, his vision beginning to haze as his need to fuck and feed took over his system. With his vision altered to track the flow of blood beneath his beloved's skin, he licked his lips in anticipation. "Need you."

"Hell, yeah," Dare growled. "Love your eyes red with your need for me."

Price grinned broadly as he took the lube from Dare, pleased and relieved his shifter didn't have a problem with his irises turning red. He'd heard some human beloveds found it eerie, but not his shifter. His beloved was perfect for him.

Except the tentacles.

Banishing that uncharitable thought, Price popped the cap as he positioned his knees between Dare's. He saw the mess of seed and lube on his groin and stomach and knew that most of that cum was his own. Price couldn't wait to add to the mess.

With that goal in mind, Price poured a liberal amount of slick onto his palm. He closed the tube and tossed it aside as he gripped his cock and spread the fluid. Shivering, he couldn't resist giving himself a couple of extra jacks . . . especially when he noticed the hungry way Dare watched him.

"Ready for this?" Price teased, sliding his slick fingers down to cup his balls. "Wanna see my cum dripping from your ass."

Dare's grin appeared somewhat feral. "Then maybe I should roll over so you can mount me like a stallion does a mare in heat."

Price growled softly as that vision entered his head . . . and he didn't think it was completely his own imagination. Realizing their bond was forming—a gift where a vampire could speak telepathically with their beloved, sharing words and images—and that Dare wanted to feel that, he nodded once. His cock throbbed, and his balls rolled, so he gripped the base to stem his need for release.

"Roll over, Dare," Price ordered, easing back a little to give him room. "I'm going to fuck you into the mattress."

To Price's pleasure, Dare moved swiftly. He tucked his legs to his chest and rolled. In seconds, he rested on his front, his knees under him and spread wide, while his arms were stretched forward to grip the base of the headboard.

Price nearly gasped when he spotted Dare's gleaming and stretched hole.

"Dare," Price breathed on a moan as he slotted up behind his beloved. Rubbing a hand down his shifter's spine, he touched his cock head to his hole. "So gorgeous."

"And yours."

Upon hearing Dare's statement, Price knew he needed to make it so. "Yessss," he hissed as he pushed into his shifter's tight, wet hole. "Mine."

Grabbing Dare's shoulders, Price sprawled over his lover. He remained still for a few seconds, reveling in the feel of his beloved, his one and only, beneath and around him. When Dare whined and shivered a little under him, Price moved one arm to around his waist.

With his grip on Dare's shoulder and waist, Price gave his lover what he wanted and started a punishing rhythm designed to drive them both out of their minds all over again.

"Mmm, that's the best way to wake up," Dare murmured into Price's ear before nibbling gently on his vampire's neck.

Price's low chuckle reached Dare, and he felt his mate rub his hand over his forearm where it was still banded around his abdominals.

Dare lay on his side, spooned up behind Price. He continued to bask in the afterglow of exceptional sex, holding his mate in his arms. Even his half-hard prick remained inside Price's body, and he felt no need to pull away.

Never would Dare have dreamed that he could feel so sated while still not wanting to release his lover.

41

Gently, Price kissed Dare's other wrist — the one attached to the arm slipped under their pillows. That had allowed his vampire to sink his fangs into his flesh and drink. The resulting double-orgasm had caused spots to flash across Dare's vision.

So fucking amazing, every single time.

After almost two weeks together, Dare knew he would never get enough of Price, and he knew that was how it should be. He loathed the time away from his mate while working, but he had a job to do. At least his alpha had given him a full week off to bond and get to know Price before asking him to return to work.

Dare finally understood why Kaiser always flew to San Diego every time his mate, Arthur, had to go there for business. During those times, their pod was run by Beta William Roush, Kaiser's younger brother. While a little more fun-loving and easy-going, William was just as capable a leader.

"What's on your agenda today?" Dare asked softly, still unwilling to break the peacefulness.

"Ovram discovered General Udraum is sending military police out to question Graham today," Price revealed, turning his head to meet Dare's gaze. "I'm going to sit in a conference room with him and watch the interview."

"I'm surprised it took them so long to decide to come out here," Dare mused, gently skimming his fingertips along the lines of Price's abdominals. "Ovram must have been doing a damn fine job at getting them to chase their tails out east."

Price chuckled softly. "That he has."

Ovram was a sea lion shifter and their pod's technical guru. He'd created some kind of special array under the water around their park. That allowed them to shift and swim without running into the chance of being picked up on radar. According to Ovram, if anyone looked too closely into it, they would think it was a natural phenomenon caused by minerals in the cliffs.

While Dare didn't understand it, he certainly appreciated it. A giant octopus swimming so near shore would definitely draw attention. Plus, some of the other shifters in the pod shared their spirits with creatures that were supposed to be extinct.

"When are they supposed to be there?" Dare asked curiously.

"Eleven or thereabouts."

Dare nodded as he nuzzled kisses along the tendon of Price's neck. "I'll be at work," he murmured softly, disappointed that he wouldn't be there to support his mate. "Be careful, and stay with Ovram."

Price chuckled as he shifted in Dare's hold. His rolling to face him caused Dare's prick to slip from his body, and he grunted softly at the stimulation to his overly sensitive appendage. Then Price plastered his chest to Dare's and kissed him hard on the lips.

"I will be," Price promised. "I'll never jeopardize what we have together."

While Dare knew that, he hadn't been able to censor his words of caution. His need to care for his mate was too instinctual. Even the fact that Price, as a vampire, could take care of himself hadn't mattered.

Threading his fingers through Price's pale-blond hair, Dare smiled into his beloved's light-blue eyes. "I know. Just instinct," he murmured with a smile.

Price winked, not appearing at all upset. "If they're gone early enough, do you want to meet for lunch?" With a lick of his lips, he added, "I'd love some of that fried calamari that's served at *Mini Barrier Reef Cantina*."

Dare hummed, and his stomach grumbled at the thought of food. "Followed by their deep-dish pepperoni pizza." Dare had been so pleased to discover his mate had loved the stuff as much as himself. Upon seeing Price's wide smile and nod,

Dare urged, "Holler at me when they leave. I'll take my lunch hour then." Dare referred to the mind link he shared with Price. He loved the fact that they could speak whenever they wished to each other, no technology required.

"Deal."

After another few minutes of making out, Price pulled away and began sliding from the bed.

Knowing they needed to start their day or he would be late for work, Dare released his hold and did the same.

"So, I have a question that's been rattling around in my head for a while," Price began as he led the way into the shower.

"Shoot," Dare encouraged before standing in front of the toilet for his morning piss.

Price reached into the shower and turned on the water. "I saw Kaiser and William eating the calamari appetizer a few days ago."

Dare shook off and headed to the shower to start washing while Price took his turn at the toilet. "There's not a question in there," he commented as he grabbed the soap and began lathering up.

"Well, they were eating calamari, but they're squids," Price pointed out as he stepped into the shower beside him. As Dare handed him the soap, his vampire asked, "Isn't that cannibalism?"

Unable to help himself, Dare chuckled as he shook his head. Using the soap still on his hands, he began rubbing Price's skin. "No, my mate. We're shifters, not animals. We're a completely different species."

"Oh." Price's brows furrowed as he nodded slowly, absorbing that information. Absently, he began returning the favor and washing Dare. "I guess that's good. Otherwise, cow shifters could never eat a T-bone steak."

Dare had learned over their short time together that a T-bone was Price's favorite cut. "Yeah. Although, from what I hear, many cow shifters and other prey animal shifters do end up leaning toward the vegetarian side of eating than predator shifters."

"Huh." Price nodded again. "Guess that makes sense," he conceded. "After all, you guys do take on certain traits of your animals." He lifted his arms and rubbed up Dare's neck to his head. "Like how you're bald."

His vampire had finally asked about that after living together for four days, pointing out that he'd never seen Dare shave his head. He'd explained that the only hair on his body was the very thin bush around his cock. His lover had admitted to thinking Dare man-scaped, which had caused him to laugh.

After their shower, Dare dressed for work in a *World of Aquatica* security polo, jeans, and hiking boots. Giving his mate a kiss, he'd murmured, "I look forward to seeing you soon."

Price nodded. "Have a great day, and stay safe."

Dare winked. "Always."

CHAPTER SIX

Sighing deeply, Price settled on the edge of the sofa and stared at the closed door. He wouldn't admit it to Dare, but he was bored out of his mind. After adolescence, never in his life had he not had some sort of job.

"And now I sit at home like the little wife," Price grumbled.

Price propped his elbows on his thighs and rubbed his face with his palms, knowing that wasn't a fair assessment. He was in hiding, after all. It wasn't as if he could spend the day working security or waiting tables.

"Not that I'd want to wait tables, but security could be good." Price flopped back, resting his head on the back of the sofa. "And now I'm talking to myself."

Peering to the left, Price checked the clock hanging on the wall. He saw it was only half-past eight, which made sense. His beloved's shift started at nine.

Feeling restless, Price rose to his feet. He headed into the kitchen and began cleaning up the remnants of their hurried breakfast. It was a good thing neither of them ate much in the morning, or they would have to start waking up earlier to accommodate their morning fucks.

Price closed the bag of bread and placed it in the breadbox. The toaster went into the pantry, and the butter was returned to the fridge. He grabbed a sponge, turned on the water, and soaked it before wiping down the counter.

After Price rinsed the dirty sponge, he placed it on the edge of the sink. He washed and dried his hands, then turned and rested his butt against the edge of the counter. Sweeping his gaze around the room, he looked for something else to do.

Returning to the bedroom, Price stripped the sheets. He gathered up their other dirty clothes and piled them all in a basket. After tracking down the laundry detergent, he headed out of their suite and took the elevator to the main floor.

Heading to the back, Price found the huge, industrial-sized laundry room. The space housed a dozen washing machines and twenty dryers. He nodded and greeted the two women already utilizing some of them before getting his own loads started. Then he settled on a chair to read a book.

Hey, Price?

Price wasn't certain how much time had passed when he was pulled from his book by the sound of Dare's voice in his head.

Smiling, he responded. *Hi, beloved. How's your day going?*

Fine. Dare sounded concerned, even in his head. *But Ovram said you're not picking up your phone.*

I'm in the laundry room and didn't bring it down. Price realized one of his dryers was done, so he rose to his feet. *Did Ovram tell you what he needed?*

The military police were dispatched early. They should be there in the next fifteen minutes. Hurry, if you're going to make it to the observation room.

Damn. Price yanked out the sheets and shoved them into the basket. He checked the time on the other dryer, relieved to see it would go off in two minutes. *Tell him I'll be there in five minutes.*

Price realized it was a good thing the small conference room was just down the hall. He figured Ovram wouldn't care that he had a basket of clothes with him.

I'll let him know. Why are you doing laundry?

Grimacing, Price admitted the truth. *I'm used to being active, my beloved.* Staring vacantly at the timer, he shoved his hands into his pockets. *I've always had a physical job. This is the first time I've been forced to lie low. I'm more than a little bored.*

Oh, my mate. I'm so sorry. Dare's remorse came through their link. *I should have thought of that. We'll meet up with the alpha and see if we can't find something to keep you occupied.* Then a soft snort touched Price's mind. *No wonder our condo is always spotless. I was thinking maybe you were a neat freak, but now I know better.*

While I do like things tidy. Price opened the dryer as the timer was buzzing. *The boredom is definitely the real reason behind our clean rooms.* He didn't want his beloved to feel bad. After all, Price was partly to blame. He could have said something. *I should have let you know I was restless, my beloved. We'll sort it out.*

We'll talk about it tonight.

Price smiled upon hearing Dare's vow. *Looking forward to it. I'll let you know when the military police leave.*

See you for lunch.

Grinning, Price picked up the laundry basket and headed out of the room. *Count on it.* Then he made his way to the conference room.

After a perfunctory knock, Price opened the door. He spotted Ovram at the table with a laptop set up in front of him. The large screen used for projecting presentations had been pulled down, and there was a picture of Kaiser's empty office on it.

"Hey, Price," Ovram greeted, turning away from whatever he was doing. "Glad you could make it."

"Thanks for having Dare get in touch with me," Price replied, setting his laundry basket down by the wall. He locked the door behind him, then headed toward the table. "Lost track of time in the laundry room and hadn't bothered to take my phone."

Ovram nodded as he returned to his laptop. "Well, they're coming to the gate now."

The view on the large screen changed to a paved driveway

and a gated entrance where an unmarked SUV was pulling to a stop before it. As Price took a seat in one of the comfortable chairs, he saw the driver's side window roll down, and someone leaned through the opening. He pushed a button, and a buzzer sounded in the room.

Price arched a brow in silent question as Ovram grinned broadly and winked at him. He leaned toward his laptop and pushed a button.

"World of Aquatica Condominium Security," Ovram stated. "How can I help you?"

"You can open the gate," the man in the SUV replied brusquely.

"I'm going to need your name, sir," Ovram replied evenly. "As well as who you're here to see."

"I'm Major Richard Barkley, with South Maxin Air Base's military police," the man claimed, annoyance clear in his tone. "And I'm here to see Graham Canton."

Ovram grinned at Price and whispered, "Let's annoy him a little. What do you think?"

While Price didn't think annoying anyone in the military was a particularly smart idea—better to get them in and out as quickly as possible—he kept his opinion to himself.

"Of course, Major Barkley," Ovram said into his laptop. "Please hold up your military ID so I can scan it and confirm."

The major looked more than a little irritated, but he did it.

"Thank you, sir," Ovram continued in an even, steady voice. "Please wait where you are, and I'll have security to you momentarily to escort you."

"Why do I need an escort?" Major Barkley demanded. "You hiding something in there?"

Ovram smirked, but his amusement didn't bleed through into his tone. "I'm sorry, sir. Standard procedure," he claimed. Then, since no one wanted the MPs to know they'd been expected, he lied, "I'm also having security contact Graham, since currently, he's at work. It'll be just a few minutes to get him, so they'll escort you to a comfortable office to wait."

The major didn't look pleased, but he responded with a, "Very well." Then he rolled up his window.

"Can you zoom in on him?" Price asked, something about the man niggling at him.

"Sure." Ovram did it, blowing up the major's face on the screen.

Price frowned as he searched his memory for what was bothering him. The slant of the cheekbones, the hue of dark hair, and even the cut of his eyebrows all tugged at Price's subconscious. Finally, it hit him, causing him to suck in a surprised breath.

"Well, damn," Price whispered, feeling his cheeks heat. "When did he change careers and get promoted?"

"You know him?" Ovram asked curiously.

Nodding, Price admitted, "He was a one-night stand four years ago on a station overseas." He wasn't about to share more details with the tech-savvy shifter. "He called himself Rich that night, and I said I was Pierce. I hope it's just a coincidence that it's him."

Ovram scoffed and began typing away on his laptop. "Price, I don't believe in coincidences."

Sadly, neither did Price.

"We have a wrinkle. Come with me."

Dare turned to face Kaiser. His alpha was already beckoning, so he started toward him.

"What is it, sir?" Seeing as Dare was in the middle of a crowd, the sir honorific was the best he could do.

"The cart is this way," Kaiser replied without answering.

With an impending sense of déjà vu, Dare hurried after Alpha Kaiser and his long stride. He appreciated his own six-foot-six frame because his alpha was in a hurry. Once they were in the cart, Kaiser drove a bit faster than he normally would through the park, using back ways that traditionally didn't have as much traffic.

Once they were clear of the park proper, Kaiser stated bluntly, "One of the military police is a prior one-night stand of your mate's."

Growling softly, Dare grumbled, "Well, he's not going to get him back, and he's not going to take him in." Kaiser grunted, so Dare pressed, "Why is this a wrinkle?"

"Because Ovram discovered that Richard, that's the guy's name, put in a transfer to the military police at the first available opening after his interaction with Price, and now he's running point on tracking him down."

Dare groaned. "I don't believe in coincidences."

"Neither do I," Kaiser replied. "Something happened that night that either tipped Richard off to Price's non-human status, or there's some other reason this man decided to start monitoring Price's activities. Until now, Price has been squeaky clean." Turning the cart toward the condominiums, Kaiser added, "And can you guess who managed to push through the paperwork enforcing Price's surprise drug screening?"

"Seriously?" Dare scowled as he watched an SUV approach from the direction of the front gates, following behind another cart being driven by Eban. "What the hell does this yahoo have against my mate?"

"A very good question," Kaiser replied. "One I hope to find out."

Just as the SUV came to a stop beside Eban's cart, Saul strode out of another building and started their way.

Dare felt his brows shoot up. If their pod lawyer was attending the meeting, he figured his alpha expected trouble. That didn't bode well.

Keeping his mouth shut, Dare fell into step a pace behind Kaiser. He adopted an impassive expression as he remained watchful. After all, both men who exited the vehicle wore weapons.

"I'm here to see Graham," the man who'd been driving stated. "Where is he?"

"My fiancé is waiting in Mister Roush's study, Major Barkley," Eban told the demanding soldier. Eban used a hand to indicate Kaiser. "This is Mister Kaiser Roush."

Instead of offering his hand, Major Barkley curled his lip at Eban. "Graham is your fiancé?" he demanded incredulously. "He's *gay?*"

Eban narrowed his eyes as he frowned at Major Barkley. "Yes. We're gay." Moving toward the front door, he stated, "This way, please."

"Glad he's out of the military already," the major grumbled quietly to the other soldier.

That man seemed to ignore the comment in favor of grabbing the open door from Eban and holding it for the major.

Alpha Kaiser's eyebrow twitched just enough to catch Dare's attention, betraying his distaste of the man as he followed them into the complex.

Eban led the way into Alpha Kaiser's office, where Graham was waiting. While, for the most part, he didn't need a cane to get around on his prosthetic leg, he had one in hand. Putting a smidge of weight on it, Graham rose from the love seat to face their guests.

"Graham, this is Major Barkley." Eban indicated the lead man with one hand while wrapping his arm around Graham's waist with the other. Then Eban focused on the second human. "I'm sorry. I don't believe I've caught your name."

"I'm Sergeant Louis Ferrara, sir," the man replied, although he didn't offer his hand.

Before more could be said, Major Barkley focused on Kaiser, Dare, and Saul. "It was nice meeting you," he lied, even though he hadn't met everyone. "I'll take it from here."

"Likewise," Kaiser stated before moving toward a chair off to the side. Saul followed him. "Will you fetch me a whiskey, Dare?"

"Of course, sir," Dare immediately replied. "For you, Saul?"

Saul settled on another chair and stretched out his long legs. "I believe a scotch would be lovely."

Dare moved toward the sideboard. Over his shoulder, he called, "Anyone else want anything?"

"For you to leave," Major Barkley demanded. "I need to speak with Graham alone."

"Actually, you don't *need* to speak with Graham alone," Saul countered with a cool smile. "You merely *want* to speak with him alone."

"But that's not going to happen," Kaiser stated.

"Toss a couple of bottles of water our way, would ya, Dare?" Eban called, completely ignoring the military men.

"I fail to see why you are here," Major Barkley stated. "This is a military matter."

"As Graham is retired, he can certainly ask for outside representation, should he wish to," Saul stated, pulling a card from his inner pocket. "Saul Davison, at your service."

"You're a lawyer," the major stated, crossing his arms over his chest, refusing to take the card. "What would an innocent man need with a lawyer?" He pinned a cold look Graham's way. "What are you hiding, Graham?"

"When I heard you were at the gate asking for one of my employees, *I* asked Saul to be here," Kaiser stated, a relaxed smile curving his lips. "Just in case."

Dare poured the alcohol first, then tossed two water bottles to Eban. He took one for himself, too. Finally, he focused on a clearly angry Major Barkley and the sergeant, who was barely suppressing his amusement, although it dominated his scent.

Evidently, the sergeant found their refusal to follow the major's demands quite funny.

"Fine," Major Barkley growled. With an angry scowl on his face, he focused on Graham. "When was the last time you heard from former team member Price Litner?"

When they'd discussed the military police coming, they'd all agreed that Graham should stick as close to the truth as he could. "Tuesday the thirteenth," Graham claimed, which was true. "At eleven-thirty-two that morning."

"That seems specific." Major Barkley jumped on that information. "Why do you remember so specifically?"

Graham held up his phone, showing them the display with the phone number and time. "When I heard you were on your way, I looked it up." He rested his phone on his knee before Barkley could take it.

"And what did you discuss?" the major demanded.

"He told me that he had run into some trouble, and he was heading out of town for a while," Graham told the military men, lying confidently. "He told me he wanted to give me a heads up, since he didn't think he'd have internet access and wouldn't be able to return any messages."

"Did he say where he was going?" Major Barkley asked. "What trouble did he say he was in?"

Shaking his head, Graham claimed, "I asked if I could help. Price said no." He narrowed his eyes at the pair. "And no, Price didn't tell me where he was going, but I told him that if something changed, I'd always be there for him. Once a team member, always a team member."

Smirking, Major Barkley stated, "I understand that's not how Mick felt about things. He tried to kill you a while back. Didn't he?"

Graham frowned at the major. "He tried."

"And now he's missing." Major Barkley crossed his arms over his chest. "Funny how your last two surviving team members are both suddenly missing." He peered around as if he could see through the walls. "Maybe I should take a look around. Maybe they're both here and not missing, after all."

"Mick drugged and kidnapped Graham, then took him out on a rented boat, chummed the water, and threw him overboard," Eban stated coldly, sneering at the major's smirking visage. "I should know. I was there. I pulled Graham out of the water onto the back of my jet ski. When Mick tried to chase us, there must have been a boat malfunction. The engine exploded, and he went down with the ship."

"Except, no body," the major pointed out. "Maybe he's still around."

Dare barely resisted grimacing. Somehow, he'd known that not providing a body when he'd sunk the ship would bite him in the ass. Instead, in giant octopus form, he'd wrapped his tentacles around the boat and sunk it, making certain the asshole had drowned with it. Eban had saved Graham, although he'd been in great white shark form and not on a jet ski.

Eban smiled coldly at Major Barkley. "If Mick does turn up and comes after Graham again, I'll be right here to stop him." Then he turned a warm gaze on his mate. "Of course, my man can take care of himself, too, so good luck to him."

"That sounds like a threat," the major stated, scowling at him.

Smirking, Eban relaxed on the sofa and wrapped his arm around Graham's shoulders. "Wouldn't you do anything for the safety of your spouse?"

"I don't have a wife, yet," Major Barkley replied, scowling. "But I'm sure if she were ever in danger, I'd take care of it the right way."

"Any way that my soon-to-be husband and I walk away

safe is the right way in my book," Eban declared. Then he focused on Graham as he teased the back of his neck. "You're everything to me. You know that."

Graham nodded once. "I know that."

Eban gripped Graham's neck and leaned forward, placing a chaste kiss on his mate's lips.

While the sergeant didn't bat an eyelash, the major curled his lip and muttered, "Disgusting."

CHAPTER SEVEN

"Well, at least we know why he's after you," Kaiser stated dryly.

The alpha was relaxing on a love seat in a large lounge on the second floor with his arm around his human mate, Arthur. The first time the human had met Price, he'd gaped upon learning that he was a vampire. Then he'd had plenty of questions.

"Yeah, I must have popped his cherry, and now he's pissed he gave in to his desire for a guy," Price commented dryly. Hearing Dare's low growl and feeling his arm tighten around his shoulders, he rubbed over his shifter's thigh. "Sorry. That was crass. I'm just annoyed he's the reason I'm in hiding."

"Yeah, but if you never came to hide here, you wouldn't have met your beloved," Graham pointed out. He was relaxing next to Eban on another sofa. "So maybe you should thank him."

Taking in his friend's smirk, Price replied glibly, "Oh yes. Should I ever come face to face with the asshole, I'll be sure to do that." He shook his head as he thought back to that night. "What I don't understand is . . . *he* came onto *me*. Why's he so pissed now?"

"I think I can answer that," Ovram claimed from where he sat in the corner with his nose in a laptop.

When Dare growled again, Price turned his head and nuzzled his neck. "Sorry, Dare," he murmured. "I didn't mean to have some random hook-up cause problems, but Graham is right." He winked and smiled at his beloved. "If it weren't for him meddling in my life, I never would have met you." Sobering, Price admitted, "I've always stayed away from other paranormal groups because you never know what kind of leader you're getting."

Price smiled faintly in Kaiser's direction. "You got a good one, though."

Kaiser chuckled and dipped his chin but didn't comment. Instead, he turned his attention to Ovram. "What do you have, Ov?"

Ovram lifted his focus from whatever he was reading. "Oh, right. Um." Then he glanced at his screen again before addressing everyone. "So, it seems that another guy in Barkley's squad spotted him with you, Price. He rounded up some other soldiers, and they beat the shit out of Barkley." Grimacing, Ovram shook his head. "Guess the military police guy who helped bring them to justice had a few effects on him, so he followed in his footsteps. Oh, and that guy was old school, a *fags are bad* type of guy, so Barkley convinced him that the other soldier had been wrong about what he'd seen. Still, it took him a while to recover, and he must have decided he needed to get rid of all *fag soldiers*, so no one else could ever be coerced against his will like he was."

"And of course, he would want to figure out who I was and get rid of me," Price grumbled, shaking his head. "I was the catalyst for all his problems."

"So, we have a couple of possible ways of dealing with him," Kaiser pointed out.

"Am I going to want to hear this, or should I leave the room?" Captain John Casinov asked dryly. He was the human mate of Beta William, and as a police captain, sometimes he had to have selective hearing.

William rubbed John's thigh and grinned widely at his human. "Naw, we'll make it right by the law."

John smiled indulgently at William. "Right, handsome." It

seemed it was something they teased each other about often.

Price had to admit—the idea of law enforcement on their side to hide their tracks must have definitely been appealing to the shifter pod. Fortunately, the pair seemed to be making it work if the teasing and smiles passing between them was anything to go by.

"So, let me sum this up. You take this guy to a room, fuck him"—a growl entered Dare's voice, but he kept going—"he leaves, gets attacked by guys who are supposed to have his back, and he blames the whole thing on you and all gays."

Ovram hummed. "Looks to be about right." He lifted his reading glasses from his nose and propped them on his forehead as he peered at Price. "You're not the only gay guy he's rousted, though. Lots of dishonorable discharges have taken place because of him." Shifting in his seat, Ovram blurted, "And I want to meet Sergeant Louis Ferrara."

Kaiser arched one brow. "Why?"

"I think he's my mate." Ovram's brows furrowed as he quickly continued, "Or maybe someone one of those guys had been in contact with recently. I couldn't get a real good whiff from the hallway."

"What?" Kaiser growled softly. "Then why didn't you say something before? I would have introduced you before they left."

Wrinkling his nose, Ovram admitted, "I don't want it to be Barkley, but what if it is? He's an asshole." His expression turned a little dreamy as he murmured, "But Louis was stoic and calm and"—he sighed—"his muscles are gorgeous, and his skin is golden brown." Snapping out of his obvious reverie, Ovram focused on Eban. "How tall was he? Six-foot-two?"

"That would be my guess," Eban confirmed. "And we'll find a way to introduce you."

"I'm familiar with the area around the base," Graham

pointed out. "Find out where he likes to eat, and we'll find a way to bump into him."

Ovram's green eyes lit up. "Good idea." Then he tipped his head, allowing his reading glasses to slip back over his eyes, and began typing on his laptop.

"In the meantime, we were discussing possibilities for dealing with Price's problem," William reminded with amusement. "And I have a couple of ideas."

Kaiser smirked. "All right, brother. What's your ideas?"

"I hate this idea," Dare grumbled.

Price squeezed his upper arm. "It's fine," he assured. "I'll be fine."

"You're faking your death," Dare countered. "And I'm the one who's supposed to do it."

"But you won't, and we both know it."

Dare did know it. There was no way his octopus would ever put his mate in danger. The problem was, Price hadn't even met his animal, yet.

With Price's fear of tentacles hanging over their heads, they'd kept putting it off.

Still, they needed the military police off their back. Barkley had been back to the complex twice in the last eight days. He would drop in unannounced, demanding to speak with Graham.

At one point, Barkley had had a court order with him, allowing him to seize Graham's phone and any other electronics he used. While they'd given the man Graham's phone—Ovram had made certain there was nothing incriminating they'd be able to pull from it—Saul had stopped the human from getting any other electronics. After all, technically, all the laptops and other devices Graham used were the property of *World of Aquatica.*

One good thing that had come from the moron continually popping in was that Ovram had confirmed the dick wasn't his mate.

Everyone had breathed a sigh of relief at that.

Still, they needed to deal with Barkley and his vendetta before they ventured close to the base so Ovram could pursue the sergeant.

That meant making Barkley believe Price was dead . . . or killing or trancing Barkley. The former option was the easiest. The others would require assistance and tampering with other agencies.

Due to the fact that they didn't want to bring search and rescue people — or monster hunters — anywhere near their location, they had to find a different suitable site. It had taken a few days, but finally, Ovram had found an optimal spot. They'd chosen a place in Alaska. With the area being so remote, it would be easy to believe that Price was hiding out there.

"Everything will be fine," Price assured again, rubbing over Dare's bare shoulder. "The bait has been sent, and I believe in Ovram's skills. No one will figure it out."

"Gods, I do love your faith in my people."

Dare wished he felt the same. Never before had he doubted, but never before had it been his own mate on the line. Instead, he'd always been helping another shifter.

Gripping Price's shoulders, Dare gently rubbed his thumbs over the pulse point on each side. "Don't take any unnecessary risks, and remember — "

"I know. I know," Price assured with a smile, resting his hands on Dare's chest. "You're completely cognizant in animal form." Smirking, he added, "You do remember that, not only am I a vampire, but I've been doing dangerous missions as a Navy SEAL for a couple of decades." Holding Dare's gaze steadily, he stated, "I've got this, and I have faith in your abilities, too."

"Thank you," Dare whispered. Dipping his head, he pressed a soft kiss to Price's lips. He knew they didn't have much time, however, so he kept it chaste and light. Smiling down at his vampire's flushed face, Dare knew it hadn't been enough for his mate, either. *Later.* "Remember, Pisces will be on the hill overlooking your position. If anything goes wrong—"

"Signal by removing my hat and putting it in my left back pocket," Price finished. Smirking, he shook his head. "Give me another kiss. Then get out of here. The sooner you leave—" Price paused and arched his brow.

Sighing deeply, Dare finished, "The sooner you can get into position, Barkley will come, and you can fake your death, getting clear of the asshole."

"Right."

Then Price wrapped his arms around Dare's neck. He used the hold to press his fingertips into his nape and urge him to lower his head. Going with the motion, Dare sealed his lips over Price's.

Dipping in his tongue, Dare enjoyed a slow, exploratory kiss. When his lips tingled, his cock throbbed, and his lungs screamed, he broke the kiss. Looking into the pale-blue eyes of the other half of his soul, he prayed to whatever gods cared to listen that nothing would go wrong.

"I'll never purposefully hurt you," Dare whispered before swallowing hard. "No matter what."

"I know," Price murmured back. Then he released Dare's neck and eased back a step. "See you soon."

Dare nodded and let go of Price's hips. After staring for a few more heartbeats, he turned and headed toward the shoals. The hairs on his nape stood on end, but he knew he couldn't turn to look. If Dare did, he feared he wouldn't be able to leave — the plan be damned.

Once Dare reached the silty, rocky water, he strode along the edge. His boots were soaked through before he reached the rocky outcropping he wanted. He didn't feel it though, as his animal — a beast that thrived in cold-water climates — cushioned him from the impact.

"Try to relax, Dare. Your mate will be fine. We're all behind you."

Spotting William crouched behind some bushes, Dare made his way to the beta. "I know," he replied, abashed. "I just . . . fuck. I don't know what I'd do if—" Dare rubbed his palm over his scalp, not wanting to even finish the thought.

"You're not alone in those feelings, Dare," William assured. "And nothing will happen to your mate." He gripped Dare's shoulder and urged him down. "None of us will allow it." Holding Dare's gaze, his green eyes filled with a seriousness they often lacked, William rumbled, "Have faith in your pod-mates."

Dare nodded. "Yes, Beta."

William swept his gaze over his face for a few more seconds before jerking a nod. "Good. Now, let's sit back, relax, and get comfortable." Easing onto his rear, he pulled a bag of jerky from his inside pocket. "No telling how long it will take for Barkley to show up."

"How can you believe it will just be him?" Dare asked, taking a piece of the peppered, dried meat.

Scoffing, William scowled in the direction where Price now rested on a blanket on the beach. He had a basket beside him with a deep-dish pepperoni pizza sitting on top of it, an open bottle of wine rested in the sand, and he held a plastic goblet in his hand. The vampire stared out to sea, but Dare would bet his mate listened to every sound around him.

"Because his hatred of himself, his interaction with Price, and Price himself, has been festering for four years," William stated sagely. "He's going to want a chance alone with Price, to tell him all the reasons he's an abomination and how he'll never allow him or fags like him to ruin the lives of other soldiers."

"Uh, should I ask how you can be so certain of that?" Dare asked worriedly. "You're sounding a little bitter there."

William's eyebrows shot up as he focused on him. "Damn. Sorry about that." He chuckled as his smile turned wry. "Guess I've heard one too many hate speeches from those trying to roust John from his captain's position."

Dare had heard through the grapevine that some of the other officers, as well as a few powerful men in Sacramento, were trying to get John removed. Fortunately, so far, their efforts had all been thwarted by Saul, as well as policies of zero discrimination and plenty of others who supported them. The pod did all they could to make certain their own antics could never be used against John.

"Well, I hope you're right, Beta," Dare commented, trying to lighten the mood. "I'd hate to have to rescue my mate from a military truck or train, but crashing one into the water might be a fun distraction."

William chuckled as he nodded. "That would be a lot of fun," he declared, patting him on the shoulder. Lifting his fingers to his ear, he squinted into the distance, listening to his earpiece. Then William turned and offered Dare a tight smile. "Well, I was partially right," William stated with a grimace. "Barkley brought Louis Ferrara with him."

"Aaaah, fuck."

CHAPTER EIGHT

Over the crashing of the waves, Price could hear murmuring. Even his sensitive vampire hearing couldn't make out the words, but he knew the sound of his beloved. He should have known Dare wouldn't go into the water until he was confident the plan was underway.

Price smiled, completely okay with that.

Gods, my beloved is a sweet, kind man.

Lifting the plastic wine goblet to his lips, Price took a sip. He swirled the smooth burgundy over his tongue's taste buds as he thought about his life. For so long, he'd just been existing. Finally, he had a future, a reason for living.

No way in hell would Price allow a one-night stand, even one who ended up injured because of it, to take that away from him. He'd served his country for over a century, and now he wanted a little something back. He would deal with Barkley, then spend the rest of his days building a life with Dare.

"You don't have anything to be smiling about, Price Litner." Price recognized Richard Barkley's voice, but he didn't turn right away, allowing the man to continue. "Looks like you've run out of continent."

The major snickered at his own dumb joke.

"Major, are you certain that's Price Litner?"

If Price hadn't been a vampire, he wouldn't have heard the speaker.

Well, shit. What is Ferrara doing here?

That could cause problems, since Ovram and his sea lion

were an integral part of making the narrative believable to the townspeople.

Turning on the blanket, Price took in the two men. Both were out of uniform, probably trying to blend in as tourists. He saw the sneer on Barkley's face and the concern on Ferrara's.

Price returned his focus to Barkley. "Hey, Rich. Heard you were looking for me." He took a sip of his wine, wondering what the man would say.

"You're under arrest," Barkley declared, stalking forward in what he probably thought was a slow, dramatic way.

Does he expect me to run? Little does he know.

"For what, Rich?" Price countered. Leaning back, he placed his free palm on the blanket for balance. Price rested his goblet on his upturned knee as he tilted his head to the side. "For being gay? I'm pretty sure you would be arrested right along with me."

"I'm not gay!" Barkley screamed, his face turning an interesting shade of red. "You coerced me. You raped me. I never wanted anything you did to me!"

Price felt true sadness and sympathy for the confused, brain-washed human before him. Over four years ago, he'd been shy but more than willing to explore his sexuality. Now the man feared his own nature.

If this all works out, maybe I'll try to find a way to help him get therapy . . . discreetly, of course.

"Rich, I was sitting alone that night," Price began slowly. He hadn't needed to feed, and he'd just been there to sit and relax with a beer. "You walked into that bar, and you came to me. You flirted with me, bought me a drink." Price hadn't wanted to embarrass the young, impressionable human. Plus, it had been flattering to be singled out. "You were looking for guidance, and I offered that . . . for one night."

Price had been clear. He would be happy to introduce Rich to the pleasures of gay sex, but he was shipping out in the morning. Rich had said he understood, and when Price had woken only two hours after falling asleep, the human had been gone.

Never could Price have guessed that some of Rich's own servicemen would jump him two blocks from the motel. If he'd known, he would have helped him. No one—man, woman, or other—deserved to be beaten for their nature, something completely out of their control.

"Y-You tricked me," Barkley claimed, doing his best to stick with whatever skewed memory he had in his mind. "I w-would never have—"

"What you would or wouldn't have done is besides the point, Rich," Price cut in, suddenly feeling sad and tired. "All that matters is what happened. I'm so sorry that you were attacked after leaving my room. If I'd known, I would have stopped them, but I didn't."

For a few seconds, where Rich stood there with a lost look on his face, Price actually thought he'd gotten through to him. He should have known better however. Just as quickly, a stony expression darkened Rich's features.

"What happened back then is irrelevant," Rich claimed loudly. "You falsified bloodwork. I bet you're diseased just like every other *fag*, and you're trying to hide it. I'm taking you in, and after tests, you're going to get a dishonorable discharge." A twisted smile curved his lips. "Just like all your kind deserve. *Fags* shouldn't be in the military. They shouldn't be allowed to live at all, and you'll get what you deserve. Nothing!" Sneering, Rich continued, "No benefits, no severance package, and no government assistance."

"Uh, Major Barkley?" Sergeant Ferrara began hesitantly. "Our job is to—"

"Don't tell me our job," Rich roared. "I know our job." He pulled a gun from beneath his bulky winter coat and pointed it at Price. "It's to bring in vile criminals like this one." When

Ferrara didn't react swiftly enough, Rich ordered loudly, "Go cuff him, Sergeant."

The sergeant jolted as if smacked. He pulled a set of cuffs from a pocket as he started toward Price. With an apologetic tilt of his lips, he ordered, "Please stand up and turn around, Litner."

Price knew that was the cue, so he did as he was told, setting his wine goblet in the sand and getting to his feet. When he turned, he wasn't surprised to hear a sea lion bark. That stopped the pair in their tracks. Pretending interest, Price half-turned toward the approaching animal as he kept a sharp eye on Rich.

"Holy shit," Ferrara muttered. "Is that a . . . a sea lion?"

Considering not everyone would recognize the animal that waddled around a rocky shoal and into view, Price had to give Ferrara props. "It is," he confirmed. "You don't see too many around here. I wonder if he's lost."

"How do you know it's a he?" Ferrara asked curiously.

Price smiled, pleased the man seemed interested. "Well, look at the size," he stated, pointing. "He's probably two-thousand pounds, not to mention that mane on him. Definitely a male."

"Who gives a shit," Rich snapped. "Now cuff Price."

As Ferrara continued toward him again, something long and slender slithered from the ocean.

Unable to help himself, Price froze. He was so still, Ferrara had actually started to wrap the first cuff around him by the time he yanked himself out of it. The sharp barking of Ovram in sea lion form helped, too.

"What the hell?" Ferrara whispered.

Price jerked free of the stunned human's grip.

Rich roared, "Freeze!" and pointed the gun at Price's chest.

Pointing, Price countered, "We need to get off the beach. That's an octopus tentacle."

Scoffing, Rich shook his head, "So what. It's not after us." He waved his gun negligently toward Ovram in animal form. "It's after that stupid animal." A cold, calculating gleam entered his eyes as he pointed toward the sea lion. "Why don't I stop it from moving around, and give the octopus its prize?"

"Stop!" Price called, debating whether he should sprint toward the crazy, vindictive human or not.

Ferrara beat him to it. "Leave it alone," he ordered, lunging toward Rich.

"Back off and do your job," Rich countered, actually swinging the gun toward his fellow MP.

That was obviously too much for Ovram. The sea lion barked in anger and began closing the distance between himself and Rich . . . at a surprisingly faster speed than Price would have expected. Before the pair of military men could figure out what was going on, Ovram was upon Rich.

Even knowing what was supposed to happen, Price wasn't completely prepared for it. Just as they'd planned, Dare smacked one of his tentacles on top of both Rich and Ovram, knocking them over. Another tentacle wrapped around Price's waist and yanked him off his feet.

Price barely had enough presence of mind to take a deep breath before cold water crashed over him, and the tentacle holding him was the least of his worries.

Dare had known waiting to interrupt would only have caused the situation to escalate. That hadn't made it any easier to smack a fellow shifter and grab Price. He did his best to use his tentacle to soften the way he yanked his mate beneath the waves.

Still, Dare didn't miss the way Price froze. From the way his vampire's chest hitched, he'd barely resisted the urge to suck in a shocked breath. Even the wet suit Price had on underneath his clothes wouldn't protect his face and head from the shock of the cold.

Dare carefully moved Price through the icy currents and around the rocky outcropping. He spotted a human Eban in a wetsuit waiting with an extra air tank and a submersible. Holding Price in place, Dare could only watch as Eban helped his mate into the mask.

Price gripped the submersible's handle with one hand, but signaled a desire to wait with the other. Eban nodded. Then Price turned to him.

To Dare's surprise, Price reached out and gently rubbed a palm down his closest tentacle.

It's different than what I would have expected.

Dare warbled a little in surprise.

Even around the mouthpiece, it was easy to see Price's grin.

Didn't know we could still talk like this when you're in this form, did you?

There was a definite note of teasing in his comment.

Didn't realize. Dare had a little trouble forming actual sentences with his more primitive mind, but he could get his gist across. *My mate. Safe. Well.*

Price seemed to realize his trouble. He nodded as he petted Dare's tentacle some more. *I'm good. Safe and well. You rescued me.* Then Price pointed back the way they came. *Will you go make sure Ovram and Ferrara are okay before we leave?*

Dare lowed softly before turning and using his tentacles to propel him back the way he'd come. Gripping rocks embedded in the ocean floor, he allowed his bulbous head to bob out of the water just a little. That was how he'd monitored the progress of the conversation, watching and listening.

Spotting William on the beach beside a downed Rich, he talked with a clearly confused Ferrara. The man didn't appear injured in any way. Instead, he kept glancing out to sea, obviously searching for something.

At first, Dare figured he was looking for the octopus tentacles. He nixed that idea when he spotted Ovram, still in sea lion form, lurking nearby. The other shifter peered between rocks and watched William helping the MPs.

When Barkley came awake with a shout, Ferrara practically had to restrain him, or he would have charged into the ocean. Evidently, watching the object of his obsession being swept beneath the waves, permanently out of his reach, had broken something inside the human. He yelled obscenities and screamed about how he wanted search and rescue there right that instant.

Knowing it was time for them all to get out of there, Dare gently tapped Ovram's backside. The sea lion seemed to sigh in resignation. Then their tech guru slipped into the water and swam with Dare beneath the waves.

Dare had every faith that William would handle all the cleanup and the spreading of the proper story — Price Litner was dead, swept out to sea by a rogue giant octopus going after a sea lion.

Sure, there would be a search, but they would all be long gone.

Reaching the submersible, Dare felt immeasurable relief that Price remained there waiting. He began to reach a tentacle to him, then hesitated. Price smiled around his mask and gripped his appendage, tugging it close.

Happy to oblige, Dare wrapped his tip around his mate's calf, careful to keep his suckers closed so he didn't harm his vampire.

Safe. With William. All will be well.

Price gave him a thumb up. *Good.*

Then Price turned and signaled Eban that he was ready to go.

Eban turned on the submersible's engine, hit the throttle, and began shooting them through the water.

Dare kept pace easily.

Every once in a while, Ovram hit the surface for air, but he stayed with them, even with his occasional looks behind them.

A few times, Dare thought about letting go of Price's leg. Each time, as if reading his mind, his vampire reached back, gripped his tentacle, and squeezed.

Finally, they reached a secluded cove ten miles south. While Dare and Ovram shifted, Eban and Price carried the submersible from the water and tossed it into the back of their SUV. They returned with towels and clothes.

Once Dare was dressed, he grabbed Price and pulled him into his arms. He lowered his head and captured his vampire's mouth in a kiss that warmed him far faster than any garment ever could. After thoroughly mapping Price all over again, Dare broke the kiss and rested his forehead against his vampire's.

"Are you okay?" Dare asked softly, working to catch his breath.

Price smiled back at him, his pale-blue eyes twinkling in the rays of the setting sun. His fair hair was slicked back from his face with seawater, and his skin glistened with missed drops.

In Dare's eyes, Price was the most stunning creature he'd ever laid eyes on.

"I'm fantastic."

Dare nodded, straightening a little. "You, uh —" He struggled with how to put his thoughts into words. "I mean, you didn't seem to mind, um, my tentacle?"

Yeah, that made no sense.

Except, to Price, it must have.

His vampire grinned at him. "I didn't mind your tentacles on me one little bit." Then he waggled his brows as he tightened his hold on Dare's torso. "I might be amenable to seeing how they feel in the bedroom."

Groaning softly, Dare couldn't help but ask, "Really?"

"Absolutely," Price agreed. His expression sobered. "Your touch, even in animal form, is still you. I get that now." Rubbing up Dare's neck, he smiled up at him. "I love your touch. I love you. And I can't wait to experience everything with you."

Dare's heart caught in his chest for an instant before it started beating wildly. "I love you, too, my mate. Now and always."

Then with a huge grin, Dare swept Price into his arms and began rushing to the SUV. "Come on, guys. I got me a date with my vampire and a bed!"

With many chuckles and rounds of good-natured ribbing, they climbed into the vehicle and headed to the secluded cabin they'd rented.

Dare could hardly wait to get there and start the rest of his life . . . all over again.

YOU MAY ALSO ENJOY THE FOLLOWING FROM EXTASY BOOKS INC:

Chomping on the Bullet
Charlie Richards

Excerpt

As Tony Harsnen rolled his overheating car to a stop in the restaurant parking lot, he silently cursed up a storm.

Forty-five more miles. Why couldn't the damn thing have lasted just forty-five more miles?

Tony had known that bullet Shellie's husband's friend had shot at his car when they'd been fleeing them had hit something important.

That just seems to be her luck lately, and I've been drawn into it.

With a mental wince, Tony knew that wasn't fair. Shellie Desprow had befriended him instantly when he'd moved to Detroit for his new job. She'd shown him around the area, pointed him in the direction of the best pizza joints, and explained what areas that, as a gay man, he would be wise to avoid.

Shellie's friendship had been invaluable in helping him to settle in with a minimum of loneliness. It had been the first time he'd lived on his own, and it wasn't even in the same city as his brother, Jerome, who'd taken him in when his parents had disowned him at the age of fifteen. Tony had been so worried when he'd shown up at Jerome's doorstep, but upon hearing what had happened, he'd growled under his breath, muttered assholes, and made up the sofa bed.

The next day, Tony had found Jerome at the small dining room table with his laptop, looking at listings for two-bedroom apartments.

"I suppose that smoke escaping from under the hood isn't a good thing."

Shellie's quiet comment pulled Tony out of his musings.

Reaching over, Tony placed his hand over her's and gave it a gentle squeeze. "Don't worry, we'll be okay." He pointed at the restaurant. "Let's get some food and put our heads together. We'll think of something."

"And go pee," Shellie muttered as she pushed out of the vehicle.

Tony smiled a little as he climbed from behind the wheel of his sedan. Peering over the hood of the car at Shellie, he took in her stance. She had one hand on the hood and the other on her back, and she was stretching a little, accentuating her rounded, pregnant stomach.

"You could have told me you needed to stop," Tony told her before reaching into the cab and pulling the hood release. "I would have stopped."

"I know you would have," Shellie replied with a grimace and a blush. "But you said your brother's place was only another forty miles, so I was trying to hold it."

Accepting that, Tony offered, "Head in, and I'll catch up. I want to pop the hood."

"Do you think you might be able to figure it out?" she asked as she began moving her six-month pregnant body in that direction.

Tony wasn't even going to pretend to know anything about cars. "Nope," he replied honestly. "But in car shows, I've always seen people popping the hood to let out the smoke and make certain nothing is burning."

Shellie nodded, then picked up her pace.

After watching Shellie disappear into the fast food chain restaurant, Tony opened the hood. Gray smoke billowed up. He straightened and took a step backward, waving his hand to clear it.

Tony waited until the smoke cleared, then stared at the engine.

Yup. No inspiration striking.

With a shake of his head, Tony turned and headed into the restaurant. The bathroom sounded good to him, too. As he entered, his nostrils were assailed by the scent of burgers and fries, and his stomach growled, too.

With his mouth watering, Tony quickly headed to the men's room and took care of business. He found Shellie standing near the line opening. She was staring at the offerings and nibbling her bottom lip.

Tony could guess exactly what she was thinking. What could they afford? They didn't have much cash left. Tony had his debit card, but he knew that the second he used it, Shellie's ex-husband would most likely be notified of where they were. Without wheels to make a quick getaway, Tony couldn't take the chance.

"There's a deal on their whoppers," Tony pointed out. "Two for five bucks. And we can split a large fry."

Shellie smiled with relief. "Okay."

Tony started them toward the register. "Do you want bacon on yours?" He was pretty sure that wouldn't put them over the ten dollar bill he had in his wallet.

"Mmmm, bacon," Shellie muttered, rubbing her rounded belly.

Chuckling, Tony winked at her. "Totally."

After placing their orders, asking for cups for water, Tony put his arm around his pregnant friend and guided her toward a table. "Now we just need to find a phone."

"Too bad there are no pay phones anymore," Shellie murmured, her brows creasing in concern. "We could have called collect."

As Tony nodded, Shellie's brows lifted and a smile broke her features. "Sit and listen for the food." Grinning, she whispered, "I have an idea."

"What?" Tony asked even as he obeyed.

With a wink, Shellie bent and pressed a kiss to Tony's cheek while whispering, "Everyone likes to help pregnant ladies."

Tony wasn't too sure about that. Shellie's ex-husband, Barry Kondrin and his friends were proof of that. Still, he wasn't going to rain on his friend's parade.

That didn't stop him from watching like a hawk as Shellie walked slowly toward a nearby table where two men sat. They both peered up at the same time, glanced at her belly, then focused on her face again.

Shellie's smile appeared hesitant as she stated, "I'm sorry to interrupt. I'm a little embarrassed really, but, um" — she pointed at the cellular phone one of them had placed on the table — "can I borrow your phone? Mine is dead, and my friend dropped his and it broke a few days ago." Wringing her hands, Shellie peered out the window at their vehicle, which still had the hood raised. "We're having car trouble, and we need to call his brother to pick us up."

"Oh, yeah, absolutely," the dark-haired man said with a smile. "Here." He picked up the phone, woke it, tapped on it — maybe to enter a password — and held it out to her. "Let me know if you need any other help."

"Thank you so much," Shellie replied with a look of relief, taking the phone. "I'll get this right back to you."

After another round of no problems and you're welcomes, Shellie returned to their table. She took a seat and handed over the phone.

"That was awfully nice of him," Tony commented as he took it.

"Definitely."

Tony quickly dialed Jerome's number, glad his brother hadn't bothered to change it yet after moving to another state. Up until a few months before, he'd been in Texas, where they were both born. Then Jerome's best friend, Stanton, had fallen in love with a guy visiting from out of state, and both men had moved to Wyoming.

When Jerome had told Tony that he was living on a cattle ranch, he'd begun laughing . . . until his brother had assumed him he was telling the truth. He'd been shocked that his down-to-earth brother had picked up and moved without a plan in place. Jerome had even been jobless for a couple of months before finding a new one—something Tony never would have believed possible.

Except, when Tony dialed his brother's number, it rang twice before being disconnected. He frowned and dialed again, but had the same response. Growling under his breath, he muttered, "Pick up, damn it."

As if on cue, Jerome obeyed. "Whoever the fuck this is, it better be damn important," his brother snapped, sounding somewhat breathless.

"Jerome? It's Tony."

"Tony?" Jerome's voice became quieter, but Tony still heard his words. "Hang on, Cain. It's my brother." Then Jerome asked, "Is this a new number? What happened to your old phone?"

Confused, Tony wondered who Cain was, but he figured he could ask another time. When Tony and Shellie had fled her abusive ex-husband, they'd both left their phones behind. He glanced around furtively, unwilling to tell his brother everything in such a public place.

Instead, Tony lowered his voice and went with, "I'm in a bit of trouble, and I was on my way to see you, uh, to ask for some help, and my car broke down." Hearing his name called by someone at the counter, Tony rose from his seat, waving at Shellie to stay put. "I'm in Twin Falls, about forty miles north of you." As Tony took the tray of food, he gave the woman behind the counter a smile of thanks even as he continued, "I coasted into the Burger King parking lot, so we're hanging out inside."

"You're in Twin Falls?" Jerome suddenly sounded more alert. "Really?" Once again his voice lowered. "Hand me my jeans, Cain, we gotta go."

"Of course."

That's definitely a man's voice.

"Uh, Jerome?" Tony could no longer contain his curiosity. "Who's Cain?"

"You'll meet him when we get there, and I'll explain." Jerome let out a sigh so loud it came through the line clearly. "I can hear it in your voice that something else is going on, but I'm going to wait to ask."

His brother was as intuitive as ever.

"Yeah," Tony confirmed.

"And we'll both have a bit of explaining to do." Jerome sounded uneasy as he added, "Please know I never meant to keep anything from you. I just wasn't certain how to explain . . . and it's new for me."

"Uhhhh . . . okay." Tony didn't know what else to say as he took his seat. Grabbing a French fry as he watched Shellie snag one paper-wrapped burger, he stated, "Whatever it is, we're family. We'll get through it."

Geez, I hope he feels that way when he discovers the problems I'm dragging his way.

"Absolutely," Jerome immediately replied. "Just sit tight. We'll be there soon."

"Thanks, bro."

After hanging up, Tony realized he didn't know who we were.

ABOUT THE AUTHOR

Charlie started writing fantasy when she was eight, and after stumbling onto her first erotic romance at age nineteen, she realized her true calling. She now focuses on writing gay erotic romance, normally of the paranormal variety, with heroes of all kinds. With the help and support of her husband, Charlie finally fulfilled one of her life-long goals . . . move to acreage with her horses. You can often find her curled up with her laptop and a cup of tea or glass of wine, creating her next adventure. Charlie enjoys exploring the mountains of her new Oregon home on horseback, 4-wheeler, or motorcycle.

She can be reached at ch.richards2010@yahoo.com
Or visit her at www.charlie-richards.com